Je Suis à Toi

Monsters in the Dark #4

by

New York Times Bestseller

Pepper Winters

Je Suis à Toi (Monsters in the Dark #4)
Copyright © 2016 Pepper Winters
Published by Pepper Winters

Published: Pepper Winters 2016: **pepperwinters@gmail.com**
Cover Design: by Kellie at Book Cover by Design
Editing by: Jenny Sims http://www.editing4indies.com
French Translation: Eva LeNoir & Words without Borders

OTHER WORK BY PEPPER WINTERS

Pepper Winters is a New York Times, Wall Street Journal, and USA Today International Bestseller.

Her Dark Romance books include:
Monsters in the Dark Trilogy
Tears of Tess (Monsters in the Dark #1)
Quintessentially Q (Monsters in the Dark #2)
Twisted Together (Monsters in the Dark #3)
Je Suis à Toi (Monsters in the Dark #3.5)
* * * * *

Indebted Series
Debt Inheritance (Indebted #1)
First Debt (Indebted Series #2)
Second Debt (Indebted Series #3)
Third Debt (Indebted Series #4)
Fourth Debt (Indebted Series #5)
Final Debt (Indebted Series #6)
Indebted Epilogue (Indebted Series #7)
* * * * *

Her Grey Romance books include:
Destroyed
Ruin & Rule (Pure Corruption MC #1)
Sin & Suffer (Pure Corruption MC #2)
* * * * *

Her standalone contemporary books include:
Unseen Messages
* * * * *

Her Upcoming Releases include:
2016: **Super Secret Series**

2016: **The Argument (July 2016)**
2016: **Indebted Beginnings (Indebted Series Prequel)**
2016-17 **Dark Romance Trilogy**

* * * * *

Her Audio Books include:
Monsters in the Dark Series (releasing June 2016)
Indebted Series (One and Two Out Now)
Ruin & Rule / Sin & Suffer (Out now)
Destroyed / Unseen Messages (releasing 2016)

To be the first to know about upcoming releases, please join Pepper's Newsletter (she promises never to spam or annoy you.)

Pepper's Newsletter

Or follow her on her website
Pepper Winters

THERE IS SUCH a thing as perfection.

Perfection didn't mean I lived in a world where I never got sick, argued with the man I loved, endured unhappiness, or generally still acted like a brat when certain things didn't go my way.

But it did mean that all of that...

The nonsense.

The noise.

The nastiness of life.

...didn't matter.

Some people went their entire existence without finding the destination they were owed. And by destination, I didn't mean death. I meant their life partner, soul mate, and best friend.

Q was my destination.

He was also my journey.

My test.

He was *me.*

After everything that I'd lived through, after everything that I'd done, life was exactly how it should be.

Free to be who I was with no judgement, no comments, no one trying to change me.

Free.

With him.

My master.
Until he changed the rules and I lost.

Tess

"I WANT TOMORROW to go perfectly, Suzette."

Q's rescued slave girl/housekeeper (and my best friend) spun in the oversized kitchen and planted hands on her hips. "Are you doubting my powers of organisation?"

I fought my smile. "Did I say that?"

"You implied that."

Holding a hand to my heart, I said dramatically, "I would *never* say that. I know better than to antagonise your wrath."

Suzette burst into laughter, wielding a spatula from the bench. "Damn right. Never forget it."

We shared a look full of togetherness and contentment.

When I'd first arrived—shackled and tagged like a dog—Suzette had confused and scared me. Now, my life wouldn't be complete without her.

When Q accepted me as an unwanted gift, he'd not only given me himself but his livelihood and friends, too. He'd given me a family after my own wanted nothing to do with me.

Suzette placed the spatula back onto the flour-dusted bench. "If you doubt me again, I'll have to raid Q's closet and spank you with something unmentionable."

I chuckled. "Good luck with that."

She swatted her own behind with a flourish. "Who knows? Maybe I'll be better than he is with technique."

I rolled my eyes. "No one could out-do Q."

"Yeah, yeah." She snorted. "You're just besotted. He could do whatever he wanted to you, and you'd just smile and nod like a damn bobble head."

Our laughter turned into noisy giggles.

She knew me so well.

Suzette tried to come across fierce and capable, but I knew the truth. I saw past her courageous façade. She was still damaged from her past, but thanks to Q, she was healed enough to find smiles in sadness once again. Besides, she had Franco to warm her at night and chase away whatever nightmares she still suffered.

In that respect, we were similar.

We were both rescued by Q.

Both brought back to life by the man who carved inked sparrows into his chest and loved so fiercely, hungrily, angrily that to some, he was overbearingly rude and far too intense.

To me, he was utterly perfect.

"Don't piss her off, Tess. You know what will happen." Franco laughed, propped up at the breakfast bar while cleaning his pistol that he carried to protect myself and his master.

Suzette and Franco might be in our employ, but they were family. And family couldn't be trusted with something as delicate as this.

Ignoring both of them, I padded bare-foot to the walk-in pantry where Mrs. Sucre bustled about gathering ingredients for the picnic for our journey tomorrow. "Tell Franco and Suzette, Mrs. S, that if they have any more daft ideas like what they pulled at our wedding, I'll murder them myself."

Memories of having my wedding dress torn off to reveal the kinky lingerie I wore beneath made my cheeks burn. It was a day I'd never forget.

For multiple reasons.

"They know better than to do that." Mrs. Sucre smiled as she waddled past me and dumped an armful of oats and sugar on the quartz bench. "Just like you know better than to try and micromanage everything." Patting my hand, she added, "Besides, we're all in on this secret. If *maître* knew—"

"He'd better not know." I crossed my arms, dislodging her hold. "I want this long weekend to be for him. I don't want him overthinking it."

"And you've done great so far." Franco hopped off the stool, placing his cleaned firearm back into its holster. "He doesn't have a clue. Tomorrow, you'll claim a need for a picnic, and I'll program the GPS with coordinates that he has to follow. I'm still averse to leaving you without security but I know his driving and no one will be able to keep up. The rest of us will travel in the helicopter and meet you there."

Suzette drifted to his side, an adoring smile on her face. "Perhaps, we can take advantage of this semi-vacation, too."

I glanced away, giving them a small second of privacy. They didn't display affection often, but I liked when they forgot they were in company. I loved seeing the way Franco softened and Suzette shone—almost as if the protectiveness of Franco bolstered her hesitant courage while they stood eye-locked and in love.

Deciding now would be the perfect time to leave, I waved. "Fine, I'm trusting you. I'll see you in a little bit." Breaking into a trot, I deliberately left the lovebirds and my favourite cook as I dashed up the turret staircase to Q's bedroom.

My bedroom.

Our bedroom.

Even after three years, I still had trouble saying that.

This chateau was mine.

Q's fortune was mine.

The day he'd allowed himself to take me fully was the day he'd given me not only his heart but his empire and hearth, too.

Pulling out my hair tie as I strolled across the rug, I ruffled my blonde curls as I stared at the photo of us side by side still dressed in wedding finery. We weren't aware of the camera, only each other.

If anyone tried to convince me that Q wasn't capable of

love, that he was a monster with deep dark urges, that one day he might hurt me far beyond my tolerance of pain, I'd laugh in their disbelieving face.

The way Q stared at me in that picture negated any naysayers or sceptics.

Our love was unique.

And I would never, *ever* take it for granted.

"You've given me so much, *maître*." Stroking his cheek in the picture, I murmured, "This weekend, I want to give you everything that I can. Starting with eradicating the sadness that I've glimpsed once or twice in your gaze."

I didn't know what caused it.

I didn't know if *I* was the cause of it.

But I did know I would do everything in my power to dispel it.

Unzipping my navy dress, I left it pooled on the carpet where Q had first strung me up. The night he'd come to me drunk, (after the police had interrogated him) he'd shown me exactly what I needed. It was one of my most favourite memories.

My skin tingled from that night as I made my way to the large arched window in my black underwear.

The long driveway spiralled into the manicured trees and the gatehouse hidden just beyond. Snow twinkled on bare branches, but the light dusting on the fountain and grass had thawed with the afternoon sun.

Winter.

Q's favourite season when everything died, only to be reborn fresh and bright and new. If he were here now, I'd show him just how he'd transformed me as well as any season. However, he wasn't due home for another few hours. He was working too hard—on both his property business and our charities.

My eyes drifted to the left where a new residence had been erected early last year.

We still rescued women. Still funnelled vast quantities of

wealth into our organisations—both law-abiding and mercenary driven—and shared our home with wraiths of sexual abuse.

Only now, the women we fought to repair no longer had to exist here on their own. Those who couldn't stomach to see their family so soon were permitted to remain in our chateau in a wing especially for them as long as they liked. However, those who didn't hold such deep emotional trauma were relocated to the mansion beside ours where multiple families could live and recover together.

The moment Q found another survivor, I was in charge of tracking down her parents or loved ones and encouraging them to come and be there for their daughter, wife, or sister.

Many people tried to compensate us financially. However, we refused every euro.

Our repayment was watching a terrified abused woman learn to laugh and smile again. Our reward was when they eventually left our sanctuary and returned to a world that'd almost ruined them.

Q had saved so many people.

I'd saved him in return.

But he was hiding something from me.

And by the end of the long weekend, I would know exactly what it was and how to cure him.

After all…what were birthday celebrations for if not to interrogate and infiltrate the thoughts of the birthday boy?

Picking up the photo and placing a quick kiss on his handsome face, I whispered, "Happy birthday, *maître*. Get ready to let me into that gorgeous mind of yours because I won't stop until you confide in me."

I WAS USED to sneaking around.

I'd done it as a kid. I did it as an adult. Partly because I liked to be invisible—to approach and eavesdrop when others weren't expecting and stalk the bastards who hurt women for pleasure—but mainly because it was who I was.

I couldn't change habits that had become a part of me.

I moved in silence.

I didn't know any other way.

However, tonight I wasn't infiltrating an enemy's den; I was returning to the woman I loved, tiptoeing across our bedroom like a fucking fugitive.

Every day, it became harder to avoid her.

She knew something bothered me but hadn't gathered the courage to ask yet. But she would. It was only a matter of time.

But that time was not tonight. Not after the long day I'd had.

My eyes adjusted to the dark; only a sliver of moonlight cracked through the haphazardly drawn curtains.

My wife—I'd never get tired of that word—lay balled up beneath the covers of our enormous bed.

I sighed heavily at the blonde curls (that I'd fisted and caressed so many times) spread over my pillow. Every part of her claimed every part of me.

Her skin glowed almost luminescent in the darkness, and I

read her pinched brow with concern. Even asleep, her body language let me know she was pissed at me.

And she had every right to be.

When I'd headed into the office this morning, I'd promised her I'd be back in time for dinner. Normally, I was able to keep my promises.

But not today.

Frederick had been particularly annoying, going over reports and end of year asset consolidation as if I wouldn't be there to do it.

I'd made him CEO so I could spend more time with Tess and our charities, so why had he been so adamant about me working so hard today?

Untying my dress shoes, I slipped them silently from my feet.

I wasn't clumsy.

I didn't make a noise as I shed my clothing and padded toward the bed. Tess would never know what time I arrived home or how long I'd lain beside her.

All she needed to know was I would be with her in the morning.

Maybe then, we'd talk.

Swallowing my groan, I slipped into the cool cotton sheets and lay still, gauging how unconscious she was.

My heartbeat thundered in my ears, waiting…

When her breathing didn't change or a rustle indicate she'd woken, I slid closer, wrapping my arm around her hips and dragging her back to my front.

Some days, I woke her up like this. I bit her neck, touched her wetness, and gave her no choice but to accept me.

But not tonight.

Tonight, I was tired and in no mood to play.

All I wanted to do was fall asleep with my *esclave* in my arms and dream happy dreams.

I didn't want to be sad anymore.

I didn't want to run from my thoughts.

I should be happy.

I *was* happy.

I had everything I could ever want.

Not everything.

Gritting my teeth, I cast aside such undermining frustration and forced myself to sleep.

Tess

"SUZETTE, STOP. I can manage."

Suzette scoffed, repositioning the hamper on her hip as if it were a child and not a bulging feast with delicacies only Mrs. Sucre knew how to make. "Stop being so pushy. I want to help. So let me help."

I rolled my eyes as we made our way through the back quarters of the house, past the swimming pool I didn't know existed until I'd returned to Q, and into the humongous parking garage housing prized possessions.

Q hated these cars as they'd once belonged to his father. I understood why he felt that way, but once upon a time, the chateau was his father's, too. However, ever since the day Q took power, he'd turned something grotesque in its usage into something so pure and wonderful.

Just like these vehicles. They weren't alive. They had no soul. Their lot in fate was to belong to either nice or naughty, and Q was a little bit of both.

Grabbing the keys to a limited edition Aston Martin something-or-other, Suzette and I manhandled the food into the boot. Once it was wedged in place, I slammed the lid with a muffled thump.

I brushed my hands together. "Now for the luggage and the man, then we're ready to hit the road."

"Won't he be mad that you haven't told him about this?

That everyone is in on it but him?"

"No. A surprise will be good for him."

"Last surprise he went on a killing spree to find you."

I smirked. "Yes well, this isn't a bad surprise."

"Define bad." Suzette wrinkled her nose. "Q has to be in control of everything. He hates celebrating his birthday and doesn't do well with functions run by others. You're doing all three and expect him to be grateful."

Looping my arm with hers, we traversed the garage and headed back into the slumbering house. Dawn had just crested, and our ensemble of silk and flannel pajamas were the only movable things in a home where everyone still slept.

"He'll be grateful."

Suzette snorted. "Grateful to have an excuse to flog you, you mean."

"Oh, that will come later."

She scowled. "I know way too much about your sex life."

I laughed as we stepped through the corridor and into the main foyer. "And I know way too much how besotted Franco is with you and how you want him to be a bit rougher than he is but you don't know how to ask for it."

Her eyes widened. "Hush it."

Pecking her cheek, I let her go. "How about *you* stop hushing it. Then we both might get what we want this weekend."

Leaving her gasping for a retort, I flew up the staircase to wake my master and bear his rage once I informed him of my plan.

* * * * *

My ideas of kissing Q awake and then a morning quickie dismantled into splinters as I entered our bedroom and found him stalking from the bathroom with steam curling from his skin and droplets running down his chest to soak into the towel wrapped around his sexy waist.

I'd lived with the man for years, yet I never grew tired of Q naked.

His inked skin with its birds and storms. His muscles that weren't decoration but merely talismans for a life he fought every damn day. He was freaking stunning.

I shivered as his eyes met mine.

"Where the hell have you been?" His gaze drifted to my scantily clad frame. It might be freezing outside with snow blanketing the countryside, but the chateau was toasty warm in every room. I never needed jumpers or dressing gowns thanks to Q's fastidiousness to ensure our 'guests' were comfortable after years of discomfort.

"None of your business."

A thrill tingled my spine as he stepped silently and slowly toward me. "I think you'll find it *is* my business, *esclave*."

Every part of me begged to fall to my knees in our code word for pleasure. For so long, he'd fought me bowing at his feet, saying he didn't need the submissive gesture. But now, it was all he needed to let down his barricades and free his monster.

However, his green eyes burned with a different type of passion this morning. A sweeter, less complicated desire.

I sucked in a breath as he hugged me tight. His damp hot body soaked into mine as I reveled in his embrace. "I hate waking up and finding you aren't beside me."

Pressing a kiss against his chest, I whispered, "You're getting sentimental on me?"

"You know I'm the sappiest son of a bitch alive when it comes to you."

I laughed softly because it was true. To the outside world, Q was dangerous, malignant, and someone not to piss off. In our inner sanctum, Q was my protector, prince, and lover all in one.

"I had to leave…but only because I have a surprise."

Letting me go, he scowled. "Surprise?" Dragging a hand through his dark hair, he paced toward his dresser. "You know I hate surprises. *Ne me donne pas une raison de te le rappeler . J'ai des projets pour nous ce soir et l'abstinence ne fera que les rendre beaucoup plus agréables.*" Don't give me a reason to remind you of that. I have plans for us this evening and abstinence will only make it that much sweeter.

"Plans? What plans?"

Will they coincide with my own?

Shrugging into a black shirt, he faced me while fastening the buttons.

I mourned the disappearing sight of his tattooed chest.

"Seeing as you won't share your surprise with me, I will do the same to you." His eyes gleamed as a tight smirk twisted his lips. "How does it feel to be denied something you want?"

"About the same as when you deny me an orgasm until I beg."

He huffed, turning his back to grab a pair of slacks. "And look at how such lessons have backfired."

Laughing, I wrapped my arms around his middle and inhaled the citrus and sandalwood of his freshly laundered clothes. "You'll find out soon enough." I kissed between his shoulder blades, wishing I could eradicate the tension I found there.

For months, he'd been hiding something from me.

This weekend wasn't just to celebrate his birthday, but to break whatever cage he'd built and figure out what he refused to say. He'd often said I couldn't handle the darkness inside him. I knew he still refused to fully let himself go.

It used to bother me—knowing he'd never be completely free with me. But not anymore. Because I saw it for what it was. Holding back his demons was the way Q protected me. He gave me just enough to satisfy both of us. But not enough to destroy what we held so precious.

But this…it was something else.

A secret he harboured night and day and one he refused to share even when he had me at my rawest, barest form quivering beneath his touch and open to any suggestion he might utter.

Turning in my embrace, Q kissed the top of my head. "What will I find soon enough?"

"Stuff."

"Stuff?"

"Not telling…but I will give one hint."

His face darkened. "I don't appreciate secrets, Tess."

"This isn't a secret. Besides, you're about to find out." Dancing from his arms, I headed toward the bathroom. "Oh, and you might want to pack something. Whatever you need for three days."

His jaw tightened, but before he could growl and demand answers, I slammed the bathroom door in his face.

WHAT THE FUCK was she up to?

She knew I hated secrets.

She knew surprises fucked me off and made me rage. Surprises in my world were never good. And she'd given me enough to last a lifetime. First, by forcing me to accept my darkness, and then, by being stolen from my protection.

I'd done things.

I'd killed people.

I'd hurt both her and myself.

All because of secrets and surprises.

My hands balled as I banged on the bathroom door. "*Ouvre la porte*, Tess. *Maintenant!*" Open the door. Now!

My breathing came hard and harsh as the shower splashed, echoing off tiled surfaces behind locked obstructions.

I attacked the door again. "Answer me, *esclave*. Tell me what you're planning. Otherwise—"

"Eh, sir?"

"What?" I roared, spinning to face the unwanted guest. Visitors were not permitted in this part of the house. Not even to clean. The apparatus and toys Tess and I used were for our eyes only.

People knew what I needed. Our staff and friends understood how fucked up I was. Yet knowing and seeing were entirely different things.

I shuddered as the beast inside me scratched and clawed. Tess had forced me to leave her alone. She'd barricaded herself so I couldn't lash out and torture a confession from her.

Fuck.

My cock twitched at the thought of hurting her.

The disgusting sickness never let me go. I'd already done so much to her. I'd branded her. I'd bit her. I'd whipped and bled and fucked her.

Yet now, she'd forsaken me, and the monster howled at the goddamn moon for answers to her secrets.

Franco stepped hesitantly into my quarters. "Tess said the car is ready." He rubbed the back of his neck. The guy was slightly taller than I was, yet he knew what I was capable of. He'd seen me tear a rapist's heart from his chest all because my *esclave* told me to.

"What car? *Pourquoi?*" Why? I pointed at the door, punching it again for good measure. "Know what? I'd rather hear it from her." I hoped she understood my anger at her stupid games. The moment I had access to her, she'd regret ever keeping things from me.

Franco glanced at the locked bathroom, a slight smile on his face. "Fuck, she does know you well."

My nostrils flared as my heart raced to a diabolic rhythm. "What does she know?"

"That you wouldn't take this news calmly."

I fought my temper. "Being kept in the dark won't exactly make me calm."

Things had been going so well. I had her. My work. My charities. Yes, I was frustrated, and I wanted things that hadn't come true. And fuck yes, I'd found myself curbing my true nature more and more because the longer Tess was my wife, the more I fought the need to keep her safe—even from myself. But none of that mattered because I had her. I'd earned her. Hadn't I?

Our marriage was good.

Our sex life was excellent.

But things were…missing.

No, not missing.

Changing.

"Fuck!" I roared, kicking the door, wishing I had an axe to chop it to smithereens. My attention slipped from Franco and his fucking cryptic comments to the ceaseless shower washing my naked woman only a few metres away.

Goddamn door and the extra locks and precautions I'd installed. Ever since Tess was drugged and stolen in my office bathroom, I'd had a love-hate relationship with them. Love because a shower had been the first time I'd taken her. And hate because a bath had been the last thing I'd seen before a rampage that'd ended in countless lives slaughtered and yet more blood smeared across my condemned soul.

"Eh, sir. Phone call for you."

"Quoi?!" What?!

Franco stomped forward in his work boots and shoved his cell-phone into my paw. "It's Frederick. Tess told me if you refused to listen to me, you'd listen to him."

I groaned, swiping my free hand through my hair.

I'd let it grow a little. Mainly because Tess had a fucking adorable way of holding onto it if I didn't restrain her, using the strands as handle bars as I bit her pussy and forced her high.

She'd called me a tyrant. A beast.

She was right.

But she loved it. Just like I loved giving it to her.

My eyes narrowed as Franco motioned for me to hold the phone to my ear.

Grudgingly, I did.

The second the cool device rested against my skin, my business partner and annoying best friend commanded, "Leave your poor wife alone, Q."

"Shut up. You don't know what the hell is going on, and it's none of your goddamn busi—"

"Wrong. It is my business. I've been helping Tess arrange this for weeks."

"What!?" My voice bounced off the soft furnishings. Franco had the decency to point at the exit and retreat. The minute he was gone, I paced the carpet feeling more and more as if I'd lost control and had no power over the feral monster inside.

The monster that very much wanted Tess's blood even while desperately needing her love.

"It's your birthday in two days, Q. You never celebrate. Tess wanted to give you something special. Take you away from work and life." He paused before continuing with a sharp bark. "You're going to give in. You're not going to force her to change her plans. Got it?"

"I never wanted any of this."

"I know you didn't. That's why she's done it for you. She loves you, you stupid son of a bitch. Let her show you and play along as if you appreciate her efforts rather than want to kill her for them."

I sulked, glowering at the sex harness tucked in the rafters above. The last time I'd used that, Tess had slept for twelve hours straight, recovering from our escapades. "If I agree, tell me what she has planned. Tell me. Otherwise, I won't do it."

What if she'd arranged some crazy sex game designed to give me whatever she thought I needed? What if she pushed me too far and I lost all control and snapped?

I fucking loved her. But I'd never unlocked the cage inside completely, because I didn't trust my true nature. But there was also a part of me that was very much human. And Tess was what *kept* me human while almost destroying me at the same time.

I granted her pain because she wanted it as much as I did. But just by being alive and in my bed she caused me more pain than I'd ever endured.

"No, that's where trust comes in." Frederick chuckled. "Trust her. Trust *us*. Get into the car, follow the GPS, be nice to her, smile and pretend you're having a great ole time. And then meet us at the rendezvous tonight and enjoy yourself for once."

"*Enjoy* myself? How can I enjoy myself if I don't know what's coming?"

"You know your wife. That's enough." Frederick laughed. "Go get in the car, Q. Don't make me come over there and hog-tie you."

"You wouldn't fucking dare."

"Watch me." He hung up.

Baring my teeth, I tossed the phone across the room. It bounced against the wallpaper and landed safely in the thick white rug by the fireplace.

Silence fell.

Silence in the bathroom, too.

I stormed toward the door, laying my forehead on the cool wood. Inhaling hard, I forced my temper to a simmer. *"Je suis désolé."* I'm sorry. "You can come out, *esclave.* I've calmed down."

A scratching sounded on the side of the door, but the knob didn't turn. The sweetest voice—the voice I would never grow tired of—murmured, "Pack and head to the car, Q. I'll be down soon. You'll like this surprise. Trust me."

Trust her.

For years, I'd done just that.

I'd worked beside her, slept next to her, and been inside her more times than I could count in more positions than were legal.

If this was all she asked of me, then fine.

I could trust her.

And I would fucking obey her.

Tess

WE'D DRIVEN FOR over an hour.

Past patchwork countryside, furrowed fields, and sedately grazing animals, and Q hadn't said a single word.

When I'd finally braved leaving the bathroom—wearing a grey woollen dress, turquoise scarf, and hair dried and soft around my shoulders—I'd expected Q to pounce on me. I feared he'd strip me, bind me, and force me to ruin my surprise before we'd even left the estate.

However, my cunning ploy worked.

I knew Franco wouldn't be able to make him see reason. But Frederick could. Frederick had the same sort of power over Q that I did. We both held keys to his temper, only in different ways.

Somehow, he'd managed to convince Q to wait for me in the Aston Martin with some classical French opera throbbing through the speakers and my secret picnic shoved in the back. The expensive car was too small to include our luggage. Our clothing had been sent with our guests via helicopter. The same helicopter Q had fucked me in on the way to his office for the first time.

Our last time together before I was taken again.

Biting my lip, I glanced out the window. Snow lay in banks here and there, but the sunshine had burned off the lighter frosting. Icicles still glittered on the trees in the shade.

However, the inside of the car was toasty thanks to the heated leather seats and warm breeze from the vents.

Another few miles passed, and still, Q didn't speak. His hands remained tight around the steering wheel only moving to shift gears or hurl us around a corner.

I didn't mind he drove fast even if ice decorated parts of the road. I trusted him.

I just wish he trusted me.

He didn't trust me enough to agree to a surprise, and he didn't trust me to say what was eating him. Because something was and it was getting harder and harder to ignore.

I jumped as soft fingers caressed my neck.

Whipping my head around, Q's jade green eyes smouldered. "Let me see it."

My heart pattered, but I knew what he meant.

Slowly, I unravelled the scarf from around my throat and tilted my chin so he could see. Slipping my hair over my shoulder, the full mark was visible.

Inhaling raggedly, Q traced the brand he'd seared into my flesh so many years ago. For many months, it'd remained red and ugly. Now, the skin had silvered, and it looked like a birthmark rather than violent ownership. The Q with a sparrow for the tail marked me forever as his.

My eyes dropped to his jacketed chest, wishing I could see the brand he'd let me sear onto him in return: the birdcage dangling from a capital T. His had also silvered, becoming tangled with tree branches and sparrow feathers of his tattoo.

Unless the sunlight hit my scar correctly or Q willingly pointed out his, no one could tell we'd permanently signed ourselves to the possession of another.

Taking another rattling breath, Q continued to drive with one hand and caress my brand with his other. If he'd had a bad day, or we'd argued, or things just weren't entirely perfect between us, he found his way back to me by seeing proof that I was his. Not just in the past or now but in our turbulent future, too.

Placing my hand over his, I kissed his fingers.

His eyes narrowed.

The scent of desperation and desire braided around us.

Clutching my hand, he made a sharp left turn, veering off the road and onto a gravel path. I never looked away from him as he navigated at dust-cloud speed down the track and slammed the car into park the moment we reached a shaggy field with a falling down barn and rusted tractor.

His fingers became claws, locking around my neck and yanking my face to his.

I sucked in a breath as his lips claimed mine and he kissed me hungrily, viciously, so damn possessively. I forgot we were in a car on private land in the middle of the French countryside.

My thighs clenched together as I grew wet. My breasts grew heavy and ached, and I couldn't stop my hand as it crossed the handbrake and rubbed his hard cock through his silky slacks.

"*Esclave…*" His lips turned to teeth, nipping their way pleasurably and laced with warning down my neck to my brand. His tongue lapped the silver sigil, tension slowly seeping from his body.

He breathed calmer; a soft chuckle left his lips. "God, I'm a fucking ass."

Relief made me puddle in the seat. "Not at all. I knew you'd have a hard time agreeing to this."

He pulled back, his eyes flickering from my lips to my eyes. To so many, Q wouldn't make sense with the way he needed constant reminders that I meant what I said the day I returned to him. That we weren't living a lie. That I was his, through and through. But to me, I got it.

Because I had my own insecurities.

I feared that one day my submission in the bedroom and my fight in every other facet of our life wouldn't be enough. That one day, he'd find another slave girl—rescued from abuse and a life of pain—and find her brokenness more desirable than my unflappable strength.

We were convinced of our love for one another. Yet so distrusting of it, too.

I supposed that wasn't healthy—that we demanded so much of each other when after years together we should've settled into a more relaxed acceptance. But who was to say what was healthy and what was not. Some people didn't like sex. Others did. Some people liked vanilla. Others liked blood-play and violence.

There was no right or wrong.

No guidebook on how to be a perfect wife or husband. And if there was, it ought to be ripped up because no one could know what another truly needed. Each relationship was its own mess full of faults and flaws, fighting every damn day to be worthy.

Q didn't ask why I'd made him do this. He didn't try to pry my full intentions. Instead, he let me go and cocked his head, gesturing at the boot. "Was it my imagination or did I see a wicker basket in there before we drove off?"

I forced an annoyed scowl on my face. "You weren't supposed to see that."

"I'm not supposed to see a lot of things. Yet I do."

I knew he spoke of other secrets I'd tried to hide. He always sniffed them out like the beast he said he was. Only, it was rare for me to have secrets. After all, he was the one keeping one from me. "That works both ways," I whispered. "You're keeping something from me, Q. I want to know what it is."

He froze, locking into his seat. His eerie calmness resembled a poised hunter deciding if he should strike or run. "What the fuck does that mean?"

I sucked in a breath. I hadn't meant to bring it up. Now was not the time. I retied my scarf around my neck. "Don't worry about it. Plenty of time to argue later."

"Argue?" His eyebrows knitted in an angry stitch. "You're expecting to fight with me?"

"No, but in order for you to tell me, I either have to make you so angry you just blurt it out, or cajole you so I can read between the lines while you're softer." I threw him a tight smile. "You might know me, Q Mercer, but I know you too, and I know when you're keeping something from me."

Opening my door, I unbuckled and leapt into the crisp afternoon. "But you're right. There was a picnic hamper in the back. Full of delicacies from Mrs. Sucre. Let's stop to eat…then we can keep driving. We still have a few hours to go."

Not waiting for him, I popped the boot and manhandled the picnic basket into my arms.

The sound of his door slamming gave me a second head start before Q caught me and wrenched the basket from my grip. "Give me that before you hurt yourself."

I stuck my tongue out. "It's only a damn basket. I think I can carry it—"

"Wrong. It's a job I should do for you. Stop trying to do things that render me completely useless, *esclave*."

Whoa, what?

I trotted after him as he strode toward a sunny patch in the waving grass. "I don't expect you to wait on me hand and foot, Q. That isn't what marriage—"

"Putain, tu-testes ma patience." Fuck, you test me. Q dumped the basket, spinning to grab my shoulders. "I'm not waiting on you hand and foot. I'm being your husband."

"Well, as your *wife,* I sometimes want to do nice things for you, too. To show you how much I care."

His face tightened with a mixture of lust and love. "And I love you, Tess. So stop taking away the small chances I have to be a gentleman so it at least makes it a little easier to be the monster you so desperately need."

"*I* need?"

He clenched his jaw. "If *you* didn't need pain, then I would've found a way to kill that part of myself a long time ago. I would've found a way to be better by now. But you keep making me worse by enjoying it so fucking much."

He couldn't have hurt me more if he'd stabbed a pair of scissors into my heart. "What's that supposed to mean? That I'm *forcing* you to be like that? That I make you hurt me against your wishes?" I snorted with derisive laughter. "As if, Q. You love it. You need it. If you didn't have my pain, you'd never get off." Closing the distance between us, I grabbed boldly between his legs. His throbbing erection justified my actions as I squeezed. "There…I'm in pain right now, and you're hard."

He shoved me away. "You've turned me into a fucking sadist."

"Wrong, you were always one."

"Then I've turned you into a masochist, and I don't know how to turn you back."

"Wrong again. I was always one. We haven't changed. We've accepted ourselves. I thought you were happy with that!" I rubbed at the smarting agony in my chest. "Are you…is that what you're hiding from me? You don't…want me like that anymore?"

The thought of never having the exquisite highs of a hard fought release or the delicious sensation of his teeth breaking my skin as we shed our cloaks of humanity and fucked like animals hurt me more than I could say.

I loved Q. I would take whatever he gave me. But if he took away the very connection that brought us together…what would that mean for us?

I—I couldn't look at him.

Turning, I stormed away, heading toward the barn and the wonky sanctuary it offered. Bolting past the ancient door hanging sadly on time-tarnished hinges, I managed to make it to the centre of the musty building before Q caught me and spun me around.

"Never say such blasphemy again, *esclave*." His face swam with shadows and sin. "And never run from me in the middle of an argument."

"Discussion. That wasn't an argument." I squirmed against his biting fingers. "And why can't I run? You don't like being ignored when you want answers? Is that it? Because I can tell you it sucks when the one you love keeps such—"

"*Tais-toi.*" Shut up. His lips slammed against mine. Metallic copper instantly tainted our kiss as our teeth clashed and everything else faded away.

Ripping his mouth away, he grunted, "Don't run from me. Because it makes me want to fucking chase you and hurt you and teach you a goddamn lesson for ever thinking you had the power to leave me."

My thoughts vanished.

My body took over.

Q had this power. He reverted me from intelligent woman to begging pet. I knew what was coming. I knew because I knew him.

And I wanted it.

So, so much.

I wanted it more than candlelit dinners and fancy getaways. I wanted it more than diamonds and feather beds.

I wanted it more than life.

I was an addict to his sweetly delivered agony. And he was the drug I kept returning to time and time again.

"Don't. You. Dare. Move." Q shook me in warning and stalked off toward a bench full of dirty farm supplies.

Breathing hard, I glanced around the space.

Any moment, the owner could appear. He could catch us. But that only added to the thrill.

The tethered hay bales and discarded animal halters gathered grime in the corners while sinister meat hooks dangled from the ceiling on chunky chains.

My heart raced as Q came up behind me, dragging a meat hook along the bar in the rafters with the aid of a pole. "Arms up."

I obeyed.

Not because he wanted me to. But because *I* wanted to.

My breathing quickened as he bound my wrists with something coarse and thick, yanking my arms upward and fastening them on the hook above my head.

My weight didn't transfer to my wrists, but my knees turned to jelly.

I never knew how far he'd go. When he lost himself to the dangerous haze, he forgot about things like clothes and consequences. He would sooner slice off my outfit to get me naked than worry about what to dress me in after he'd had his fill.

However, he didn't find a knife and start hacking. He merely strolled around me with a sharp smile on his lips and threatening promises in his gaze.

"You think I'm keeping something from you, Tess?"

What? He wanted to talk? *Now?* I wasn't prepared for that torment. My body was liquid. My heart a blazing inferno. All I wanted was physical demands and sky-cresting, pain-inducing pleasure.

I blinked. "Yes?"

My confirmation was a question.

He chuckled dark and low. "Suddenly, you're not so sure?" Moving behind me again, he scooped up my hair, braiding it loosely so it wouldn't get in his way.

Way of what?

What is he going to do?

I wished I could predict him. But after three years of marriage and months of submitting to his every command, I still had no idea what he'd make me do. Sex with Q was never boring. It made my mind work trying to guess what implement he'd use next.

I wasn't disappointed.

Removing my scarf from around my neck, he remained behind me, bunching up my grey dress and tying the teal scarf around my waist so the material didn't fall back down.

Winter chill licked around my legs.

I wore a garter belt and G-string, holding up black satin tights.

The tops of my thighs were exposed and the low heels I

wore suddenly weren't sexy enough for the saucy lingerie I revealed.

Q came to my front, biting his knuckles as a fireball of lust painted his face. "Fuck, I'll never get over how much I need you. How much your body calls to mine. How much your mind challenges me. How much your fight begs me to snuff it out." His eyes darkened from green to demanding grey. "Even now that doesn't scare you, does it, sweet Tess? Knowing that the entire time I'm fucking you—the entire time I'm cock deep in your pussy, and my hand is around your throat, and my teeth are in your flesh—I'm battling the urge to strangle you and make you bleed."

I couldn't breathe.

I was nothing but memories and wetness, coming unhinged by his dirty, damning words. I didn't comprehend him in English. I heard him in my soul.

Wrapping his hand around my neck, he squeezed. "And the only thing that stops me from going that final distance— that awful, sinful distance—is how much I fucking love you. How much I worship the ground you walk on. How much I would die knowing that if I ever hurt you, I wouldn't be able to live another day. *Je me tuerais si jamais j'allais trop loin.*" I would kill myself for ever going too far.

His mouth smashed against mine. Our kiss defied logic and sensibility. He pushed; I yielded. He bit; I sucked. He gasped; I breathed.

My legs well and truly gave up standing. I fell in my bindings, letting him jerk my dangling body into his, allowing him to hoist my legs around his hips and scream into his mouth as he fumbled with his belt and trousers and shoved aside my knickers.

The only warning I had that he planned to take me so fast, so quick, so uncharacteristically raw was the briefest gush of icy air on my exposed pussy before his hand brushed my clit and the smooth crown of his cock impaled me.

I groaned and came apart as he tore right through me like

a sword. He didn't stop to make sure I was okay. He didn't wait for me to adjust to his size or depth of penetration.

He merely clamped my hips and forced me to accept him.

He did what I needed him to.

I didn't need soft words and kind concern. I didn't need sweet sincerity.

I needed a man. A monster. A master to fuck me. I needed him to take away my choice because then I could give in. I could stop thinking. I could be nothing more than Tess with her Q and scream and cry and beg and pant and thrust and *thrust* on the majestic cock of my saviour and husband.

"Fuck, Tess." Q's fingers bruised my hips as he jerked me up and down on his length.

My wrists burned from the rope. Circulation ceased in my fingertips. My eyes were hazy and struggled to focus, but my body…it was alive. It was burning and crashing and so damn awake, I felt every twitch of his cock inside me, every restraint he held, and every growl he swallowed.

"You love it like this, *esclave*. You love me filling your naughty cunt. You love me taking you when you don't know if you want me. You love being denied the right to tell me how you want it." He thrust harder, making the barn echo with the slams of our naked hips. "*N'est-ce pas?*" Don't you?

I nodded. Or at least, I thought I nodded.

I bit my lip, drawing blood as insane overwhelming sensation coursed through me.

I wanted to be naked. I wanted his teeth, his fingernails, his whip and punishment.

But all I had of him was his cock. He stood rutting into me, the perfect businessman. His hair slicked back, his shirt crisp, his woollen coat sublime.

To an outsider, he looked so collected and calm. So *normal*.

But they didn't see what I did.

They didn't have access to his eyes. His soul.

Bouncing in his hold, I glared into the jadey depths. The cage inside him was open; his beast unchained. If we were at home, we wouldn't leave our bedroom for hours while he fucked me and hurt me and tried to hurt himself in return.

He'd adore me, and we'd come. By God, we'd come.

But then he'd care for me, soothe me, bathe me, and cuddle me like any gentle lover. He'd give me the best safety he could offer all while he beat himself up for ever going too far. He'd love the bruises he inflicted while wanted to bleed himself dry for causing them.

It was good that here we had to be fast.

There was no time for games. Only the barest form of lovemaking.

"God, Q…don't stop."

"Tu crois que je pourrais m'arrêter?" You think I could stop? He yanked me forward, impaling even more length and heat into me. "You think I could fucking stop with my cock inside you and your taste on my lips." His face shredded into a fierce snarl. "Fuck, Tess. I can't ever stop. I can't. I can't. I can't." He thrust into me harder and more brutal than the last. "I don't want to. I won't ever want to. Yet I should. What if I'm causing it? What if I'm the problem?"

His question filtered through the dark subspace in my mind.

What problem?

I clutched for understanding, but an orgasm spindled, demanding precedent.

I wanted to know what he meant. I needed to know what demons hounded him.

But I was in the darkness with him, and I needed more. I needed that final flare of blackness to orgasm. Only then could we talk without the angry tempest billowing between us.

Q understood.

His seductive mouth spewed more torture. "You're such a dirty, filthy girl. You tricked me into the countryside so you could, what? Fuck me in a stranger's barn?"

My eyes snapped closed as I let him manipulate and guide me; let him corrupt and beguile me. He knew words were my undoing. He knew how much I adored him saying such crude and disgusting things because afterward, he'd shower me with proverbs and promises.

"Yes…don't stop." My pussy fisted him as his cock grew thicker and harder inside me.

Talking dirty might work for me, but my God, it worked for him, too.

It'd taken a while for him to relax into it. To use verbal as well as physical tools. But he was eloquent at it now. The best I'd ever heard.

"Fuck, you're beautiful like this. So open and wet and obsessed with how my cock feels. Tell me that you like me fucking you. Tell me that if I cut you down right now, you'd get on your hands and knees and let me fuck you like the beast I am."

The image flowed through my mind.

Him rutting behind me.

My knees bloody on the messy barn floor.

Yes!

The first wave of an orgasm threatened to wash me away.

Q chuckled, feeling it, understanding without me telling him that was exactly how I wanted to finish.

"Your wish is my command, *esclave*. Just like always." With a knife—*where the hell did he get the knife?*—he reached up and hacked through the dense rope imprisoning me. The instant it snapped free, I tumbled into his arms. His cock slipped out as he swung me to the floor and shoved my shoulders.

I tripped and soared to my hands and knees.

He was rough, and I fucking loved it.

The moment I was sprawled like a dog in heat, Q slammed to his knees behind me. The clink of his belt sent heat waves and intense desire. Would he spank me or was he too far gone?

His cock speared into me as his hand fisted my hastily plaited hair.

Too far gone.

My lips spread into a victorious smile as my master and

keeper drove into me from behind. His clothed chest cloaked my back as his hips jacked faster and faster into mine. "You're such a filthy girl. Tell me. Do you like me fucking you like this?"

"Yes. Yes. *God*, yes."

"How much more can you take, Tess? How much harder do I need to fuck my wife?"

The words fuck and wife caused me to convulse.

Q laughed, slapping my ass as his pace turned frenzied. "Not much longer I think, my dear *esclave*." His rhythmic taking matched mine in every possible way. He was so fast but so fluid. Hitting the top of me every time he filled me. He forced my body high and needy.

"Maître..." My knees splayed, and my elbows gave up. My cheek smashed against the floor, pinpricked with hay and debris as Q never stopped. Heat exploded as blood smeared down my face. His fingers left bruises on top of bruises as he yanked me back over and over.

I couldn't hold off.

I came.

I came.

I came.

And when I thought I'd finished, I came again on the smoke of the first, this one even tighter and dreadfully unforgiving.

Q followed me.

His growling grunt speared my heart as his cum flooded inside. Spurt after spurt, he marked me internally just as he had externally.

As we collapsed together on the floor, him on his back and me on his chest, I struggled to rearrange my heartbeat from manic to calm.

The ooze of his release dribbled down my thigh, but I didn't care. I wasn't cold even though plumes of our breath decorated the air. I was exactly where I wanted to be.

I didn't want to move or speak, but I couldn't stop one

resounding repetitive question from ruining the moment…
What is he keeping from me?

WOULD THE HIGHS and lows ever stop?

I thought I'd outgrown this. I thought the night of our wedding and the day of our vows had cured me of this ridiculous flip-flopping of happiness and hatred.

She made me so fucking happy.

But also made me hate myself.

I couldn't look at her as we ate chilled caviar and rosemary roasted chicken on a blanket in the farmer's field. If the farmer returned in time to see the scuffmarks in the dusty, hay-riddled barn, he might have some indication that two people had just fucked in there.

More than fucked.

Fought with their souls and punished with their bodies.

My cock still twitched from residual insanity from my release. Tess always made my orgasm so much stronger. She drew the darkness from me even when I did my best to forbid it.

I wasn't the master.

She was.

Curse her to hell.

I'd wanted to be gentle. I'd wanted to make love to her rather than fuck her like an animal. Because I meant what I said. What if the reason for my frustration was because of my own issues? What if I was the one with the problem, and I was taking it out on her?

I swallowed those thoughts before I could rage again.

Swigging a mouthful of tart champagne, I reached across the small distance and caressed her raw, scratched cheek.

We sat bundled in a thick blanket that Mrs. Sucre had stuffed in the hamper, keeping us warm from the winter frost all around us. After we'd finished our episode in the barn, I'd cared for her like I always did.

Taking her so brutally meant I had to put her back together again. I'd used the wet wipes from the car glove box and cleaned the small cut on her cheekbone from the sharp hay stalks. I'd dabbed antiseptic cream on the wound and kissed her over and over again.

She tolerated my ministrations, more for me than for her. She knew my ritual of checking—to see how far I'd gone when I lost control—was entirely for my benefit. She was so strong in that respect. She let me abuse her—*begged* me to abuse her— and then required no aftercare whatsoever.

When she'd first refused to bow at my feet the moment Franco pushed her through my front door, I'd known. Known she wasn't just my equal but my empress. Someone I would gladly worship because she had more strength and courage in one little finger than I did in my entire fucking body.

My eyes drifted to her tartan-blanketed form. Beneath her dress, I knew her hips were decorated with finger marks and a few strands of blonde littered the barn floor from where I'd jerked too hard.

Apart from her cheek, I hadn't drawn blood. However, she had. She'd bitten through her bottom lip, making it puffy and red and so fucking kissable I contemplated a second round with her spread-eagled over the bonnet of my car.

Get a fucking grip, Mercer.

We'd been married for years. Would wanting her never go away? At this rate, I'd end up in an early grave from my heart popping with pleasure while inside her.

Cupping her cheek, I breathed, "Are you okay?"

She leaned into my touch with a gentle smile. "Of course, why wouldn't I be?"

I shrugged. "I can think of a few things."

She glanced away. "Well, so can I. But nothing relating to what just happened in the barn." Tearing off a piece of chicken, she chewed thoughtfully. "You know, this birthday weekend isn't just for you."

I dropped my touch, ladling another mother of pearl spoonful of caviar into my mouth. Caviar could never touch metal or silver. If it did, the texture and taste were completely ruined. The high maintenance eating habits of the rich never failed to amuse.

"What does that mean?"

Tess glanced my way; her normally guileless blue eyes shadowed with questions. "I know you're unhappy, Q." She waved me away as my temper thickened and I opened my mouth to argue. "Before you say anything, I don't mean you're unhappy all the time. But there *is* something you're keeping from me. I need to know what it is so I can fix it."

What if you can't fix it?

What then?

I sighed heavily. "There's nothing to fix, *esclave.*"

"I say otherwise." She hung her head, pouring more champagne as an excuse not to look at me. "I need you to tell me soon, Q. Before I go mad with worry."

Stopping her fumbling, I placed my hand on hers. "I know I haven't been fair, keeping this from you. But I'm almost ready to talk about it. I promise."

"You are?" Her eyes met mine.

I nodded unwillingly. "Almost."

"So you'll tell me before the week is over?"

A week?

That's all I have?

How could I put into words something I didn't even understand myself? How could I describe the longing inside me and admit I'd been lying for months, or explain the indescribable desire for something I'd never wanted before?

It was my turn to look away, glaring at the countryside and the glittering yellow sunshine. Snow still lingered in ditches and valleys but overall, winter had been too kind. A few leaves still clung to branches, and the occasional rustle of mice and voles spoke of an existence refusing to die even with temperatures teasing with freezing.

If nothing perished, nothing could be reborn.

The same mistakes and hardships would linger.

"Q..." Tess stole me back to her.

Gritting my teeth, I tore off a piece of fresh baguette. "Fine. You have my word. By the end of the week, I'll tell you."

If you don't figure it out before then.

Tess was the most inquisitive and determined person I knew. She'd probably already guessed what my problem was. She could most likely put it into words far better than I could.

In a way, I wanted her to.

Maybe then, I could understand what the fuck my issue was.

Tess

THE LAST WARMTH of sunshine faded as we drove up the incredibly long driveway of *Castelnaud-des-Fleurs*. The Castle of Flowers.

Anyone with an income as sizeable as Q's could rent this private estate—costing a small fortune for a few days' stay.

I'd found it thanks to the contacts Q had made in the property world where he'd earned most of his wealth. We regularly brushed shoulders with building officials, high-powered governors, and businessmen with money and power.

Those same businessmen were on a secret list that Q and I'd compiled of known sex offenders and traffickers. I might have found my happily ever after, but I hadn't forgotten my vow to help others. Along with our charities and regular donations to the families we'd already saved, we kept track of underground dealings and recent sales of women. Including a new trafficking ring that'd opened in Europe called the QMB—the Quarterly Market of Beauties.

Q had enlisted spies to watch and report. He wouldn't let it go on for much longer before he slaughtered those doing the buying and scavenge for those who had been sold.

We weren't bound by propriety and paperwork of the law.

We didn't stand by and let such evil occur.

Q didn't tell me much about what he arranged, or how far he had them punished, and I didn't ask. That day he'd found me in the warehouse and wrenched the heart from the man who'd broken me had shown just how dark I truly ran.

I didn't squirm when Franco told me exactly what Q had done after Frederick carried me to the plane. I didn't gag when he spoke of the gore, or lament and ask why Q had been so savage.

Instead, I thanked him. From the bottom of my soul. He'd only done what that bastard deserved, and I wouldn't ruin his gift and sacrifice by ever being weak. Q could kill every last trafficker with his bare hands, and I would stand beside him with a rag to wash away the blood. I would spread my legs for him even while he smoked with sulphur from the gun he used to exterminate such vermin.

Did that make me a monster, too?

Yes.

And I accepted that wholeheartedly.

Turning off the ignition, Q gave me a gentle smile. Whatever violence that we'd given into in the barn was sated and whatever shyness and unwillingness to talk from our picnic had been shoved away to discuss at a later time.

He would tell me.

I trusted him.

And I didn't care what it was, I would do it. Because that was what our marriage was. He took, I gave. I asked, he gifted. We were on a never-ending tug of war where we each took turns to win. But there was no losing. We had far too much happiness to ever lose.

"Thanks for giving me time, Tess." He grabbed my hand from my lap and kissed my knuckles. *"Je ne vais pas te torturer beaucoup plus longtemps. Je te le promets."* I won't torture you much longer. I promise.

I smiled, tracing his five o' clock shadow with my eyes and lingering on his lips. "Oh, you can torture me anytime you want. Just not with secrets."

A smirk appeared. "You've brought us to a castle for a few days. I'm sure they have a dungeon and some apparatus we could find a new use for."

"I don't think they had pleasure in mind when they cooked up the rack or whatever else those medieval heathens invented."

"No, but that's how history works. They create something for one purpose, but the future finds new uses. *Better* uses." Unfurling my fingers, he leisurely inserted my index into his mouth.

I shivered as the hot wetness of his tongue shot directly to my pussy.

How does he do that?

How had he somehow not only captured all my senses but became the ultimate puppet master on my body, too?

"Ah, you've arrived." A moustached butler appeared from the massive gothic front door, peering through the car window.

Q bit my finger before relinquishing my hand. "That's your cue to behave."

I giggled. "*Me* behave? I don't know what you mean. I'm the perfect example of behaviour."

He snorted as he climbed from the Aston Martin and slammed the door. His eyes danced with danger. "That's only because they don't see what I see."

The butler snapped his fingers, summoning a chauffeur to drive away our car. I didn't need to ask if they'd take care of the remains of our luncheon in the boot or if our belongings and friends had arrived.

In a place like this, things ran effortlessly—oiled by the perfection of money.

Looping my arm through Q's, I inhaled the tantalizing scent of his coat. "What don't they see?"

His head bowed; his breath hot in my ear. "They see the blonde haired angel with a sweet smile and kind voice. They see the wife of an egotistical, stubborn investor and assume you're content to let me be in charge. They don't see you as a threat."

My temper flared. "You're saying I come across meek and stupid?"

Q chuckled, guiding me into the castle. "No, my dear *esclave*. I'm saying they're fucking stupid for not seeing the *true* you. The minx who would sooner be belted and chained than adorned in silk and finery. The woman with a temper to rival mine, intelligence to run my entire empire while still asleep, and the ultimate truth."

"Truth?" My low heels clicked on the ancient flagstones of the castle. The temperature wasn't as snug as our home, but cheery fires roared in the humongous entrance hall as we traded foyer for the heart of the castle.

He hugged me closer as staff appeared from nooks and crannies to take our coats and give us a welcome cocktail. "The truth, Tess. That you own my ass. That you're the one with all the power."

My heart constricted into a lovesick knot.

"Mr. and Mrs. Mercer." A sweet looking young man handed us a goblet with some sort of concoction.

Even now, after so many years together, I still got a thrill being called Mrs. Mercer. My maiden name was gone. Forever banished. I no longer thought of myself as Tessie Snow. She died the day she was kidnapped in Mexico.

And good riddance.

"Please, allow me to show you to your room." The man bowed, motioning us to follow.

Q and I fell into step, never breaking our hold on one another and sipping the overly sweet alcohol.

Grandeur was now a part of my life. If Q took me around the world to investigate a new hotel chain he'd invested in or the exquisite residence he'd purchased in Saudi Arabia so we had a base when he worked with the overseas authorities on traffickers, I enjoyed the gilded walls and gold embossed crockery.

However, just as wealth had dulled my wonderment, so too did poverty make it so much more appreciated. Q had been mindless in his acquisitions for wealth. He'd had nothing else to comfort him while recovering slaves found salvation in his home.

His company had been his saving grace. Until me, of course.

And now that he was happy, he gave away so much. He entered slums in Brazil and built free houses and upgraded the water supply and enlisted gardeners and teachers to form a better community.

He took me with him to Vietnam where he bought badly run hospitals and fired the staff that didn't care and replaced them with top-of-the-line nurses and caregivers. He transformed bad into good wherever he went, and I was so damn proud of him.

"Good choice, Tess." Q pointed at the wall fresco and cupid decorated ceiling. "The craftsmanship is superb."

The servant took Q's impressed interest to give us a guided tour as we climbed the sweeping staircase past portraits of long-ago deceased lords and ladies and travelled down plush carpeted corridors. Sconces, tapestries, and stained glass windows kept our guide's narration busy as Q and I nodded respectfully, disappearing further into the enormous castle.

Finally, our guide stopped outside the largest wooden door I'd ever seen. It was gnarly and knotted with no decoration whatsoever. But it didn't need any. Its simplistic weathered age was all it required.

"This is your room, Mr. and Mrs. Mercer. Your guests are on the floor below. I was informed by Suzette that you would prefer not to be too close."

I swallowed my laughter.

Damn Suzette and her meddling.

One of these days, I would book her and Franco a trip and ensure an entire hotel floor was unoccupied with the veiled innuendo that they could be as loud and as adventurous as they liked with no neighbours to hear them.

Q growled under his breath. "She's always taken too many liberties that woman."

This time, I couldn't stop my giggle. "I'll make sure she

has payback. Don't you worry."

He raised an eyebrow but didn't ask. He was wise. Women business should stay women business. Just like whatever he spoke about with Frederick was his.

Speaking of Frederick.

Q opened the door to our suite while I hung back to talk to our guide. "Everyone arrived okay?"

The boy nodded. "Yes. Your guests settled in about four hours ago. They've arranged for dinner and drinks to be served in the great hall at six p.m."

"Dinner?" Q popped his head back out. "How many are attending?"

I patted his chest. "Don't you worry about that. This is your surprise, and I intend to surprise you."

His eyes narrowed. "Tess…"

"No. You will not badger me into telling you. Trust me, Q. You'll like my surprises. I know you, remember? I wouldn't do anything to make you uncomfortable."

Okay, maybe one thing…

But apart from that tiny inconvenience, the rest of the week would be purely perfect.

TRUSTING TESS AND her orchestration of the next few days—with no guessing what she'd planned—was hard. It wasn't that I didn't trust her. I just wouldn't put anything past her.

Look at our fucking wedding.

That had been ruined by Suzette and Franco thinking they had the right to strip Tess at the altar and give me the leash to her collar.

It worked because of our lifestyle.

But it wasn't their place to do such a thing. Even though I appreciated and loved them for wanting me to accept that part of me. I got it. I did. And for the most part, I was grateful. But it also made me very fucking wary about social functions run by others.

Tess sat opposite me in a gown I'd never seen. We had a seamstress and suit maker on our books, so it didn't surprise me that the gold silk clung to her figure with skilful precision.

Suzette and Angelique sat beside her at the large banquet table while Franco and Frederick sat on my side. The six of us had indulged in a decadent meal of pumpkin soup for a starter, pheasant and roasted vegetables for a main, and finished with a decadent tiramisu for dessert.

Since we'd arrived, everything had been relaxing and calm. Our room overlooked the aqueduct flowing into the valley below, and our bed was even bigger than our one at home with the convenience of a four-poster with thick swaddling curtains to cocoon us. The giant fireplace roared and was kept stoked by attentive servants, and the large claw-foot bath by the balcony would be used at some point during our stay.

The castle was quiet and straddled modern and history with seamless charm. We hadn't explored much, but there was always tomorrow.

Sipping on a fine glass of aged whiskey, I chuckled as Franco acted out the bumpy landing they'd endured in the helicopter before we'd arrived. I wasn't surprised. The valley here would've been havoc with wind thermals.

Tess and I remained quiet, letting the others do the entertaining.

The staff cleared the table, appearing and disappearing effortlessly. It felt as if we were alone and in a private sanctuary rather than a cavernous castle.

Finishing his wine, Frederick stood up, helping Angelique to her feet with a doting smile. They made a handsome couple with their svelte frames and similar features. I didn't have many close friends, but those I did, I cherished.

"Let's play a few parlour games. What do you say?" Frederick clapped his hands, encouraging us to stand.

Tess rolled her eyes as Franco plucked Suzette from her chair.

"I don't think monopoly or scrabble are what most of us have in mind tonight." Tess murmured too low for anyone but me to hear as she came toward my side.

Wrapping an arm around her waist, it came off as kind and loving, but the fierce way I glued her to my side spoke of domination and desire. "Shall we retire and find our own entertainment?" I whispered in her ear.

She smiled coyly. "I think that's a—"

"Come on. No excuses. A few games together and then we'll head to bed." Frederick in his bossiness didn't let us say no.

With a mixture of grumbles and half-hearted hesitation, he ferried us into the room attached to the great hall and motioned us to sit in the mismatch velour love-seats and wingbacks grouped together around a low coffee table. Nestled by the chairs were a whiteboard, markers, and other paraphernalia.

"What the hell are you planning, *mon ami*?" I asked, reluctantly letting Tess pull me onto a love-seat with her.

Angelique answered for him, tugging her long dark hair over her shoulder. "Well, we're in a castle. We thought it would be fun to play some of the parlour games that would've been their entertainment back in the day."

I groaned dramatically. "I'd much rather drink." I pinched Tess beside me, hissing in her ear. "And then play with you."

She swatted my hand, fighting a smile. "Behave."

Franco hopped up, grabbing a top card from some moth-eaten time-stained deck on the coffee table. "Great, I'll start." He read the script on the chosen paper, his forehead furrowing. "There's a game called Wink Murder." Glancing at us, he added, "But I don't think we can play it with so few numbers."

"How does it go?" Suzette asked, smoothing her pale blue dress with silver lace in the panels around her chest. I loved seeing her so normal and content. I never asked her to wear a uniform while working at the chateau, yet she did.

I supposed it might seem odd to be fast friends with my housekeeper, but I found it perfect. She knew my secrets just by living under my roof. What better way to keep those secrets hidden than by befriending her and her partner?

Besides, Franco would give his life to keep me safe. And I would do the same for him, even if it wasn't in my job description. His friendship was what bought me his loyalty, not his paid service.

"One of us is assigned the role as a murderer and can kill others by winking at them. If they're spotted winking, they lose. But if they don't, and people keep dying, they can win by killing off everyone before they're caught."

I looked at our small group. "I hardly think six will work. Next."

Slapping the card onto the table, Franco picked up another. He put it straight back down again. "The Minister's Cat. I don't get the rules. I've had too much to drink." He laughed. "Brain cells are on holiday."

Suzette plucked one from the deck, pursing her lips. "This might be fun? Consequences. We each have to name an adjective, a verb, and—"

"Sounds like homework. Next." Frederick chuckled. It was his turn to grab a card. "No, not this one, either. Way too complicated."

Seemed like historical games were a lot more tricky than the games of today. Or we were just less intelligent.

Or drunk.

I'd go with the drunk option. And was perfectly fine with that.

Taking another sip, I let them decide our fate.

All I needed was Tess beside me and the expensive whiskey in my glass. My evening was complete.

"Oh, this one sounds good." Suzette held up her selection. "Charades."

We all groaned in unison.

"That's a sure-fire way to make a fool of yourself," Frederick said.

"Then it should be easy for you," Angelique quipped.

Frederick rolled his eyes. "Fine, woman. But wouldn't you much rather play that game where you have to guess the name of a movie or song with pictures?" He pointed at the whiteboard. "That's what that's for, right?"

Angelique shook her head. "They wouldn't have had that wipeable thing back then. Charades are much more in keeping with the times."

I swallowed a mouthful of whiskey, joining in the bullying toward my CEO. "Go on, Frederick. You're up. Make a fool of yourself."

Franco laughed while Tess snuggled deeper into my side.

Standing, Frederick proceeded to do exactly what I demanded.

He made an absolute utter fool of himself.

For the next few glasses of alcohol, we laughed at each other's expense.

And I slowly forgot why I was terrified of surprises.

* * * * *

Midnight chimed in the large grandfather clock in the foyer, clanging through stone walls and architraves, echoing in our alcohol-mellowed bodies.

For the past few hours, we'd drank, joked, humiliated ourselves, and hung out like any normal group of friends. Half-way through the charade skit, while Tess scratched the top of her head and blew bubbles like a monkey, I pressed pause on this magical evening and let myself enjoy such simple but valuable things.

I'd never once played like this.

Innocently played with others without barking orders, running companies, or fighting unfairness on behalf of those who'd suffered so much. Even with Tess, I was still aggressive and overbearing and never just relaxed enough to laugh and be normal.

But this...

This 'forced upon me' holiday where my work colleagues and staff became trusted parlour game enthusiasts, I was struck by how beautiful it was. How rare and fucking precious.

For the past fifteen minutes, we'd finished teasing and poking fun and sipped contently on our rapidly depleting reserves of whiskey and wine.

I was inching past tipsy to drunk, but I wasn't pissed at the lack of motor skills and slight blurriness of my vision. It was nice to be intoxicated and have nowhere to be, no worry to feel, and no one to keep appearances for.

Even in our own home, Tess and I could never let down our walls entirely because we always had guests. Women from rapists and slaves from imprisonment. If they saw us laughing and drinking, it would be a slap in the face of their unhappiness.

Frederick stretched, covering his mouth as he yawned. "We're getting old if we can barely last past midnight."

Tess giggled. "Speak for yourself. Suzette and I are years younger than you lot."

Younger by calendars but not by wisdom. If anything, Tess surpassed me in emotional intelligence and wisdom on a daily basis.

"How about one more game and then we retire?" Frederick asked, reaching once again for the deck of cards.

No one complained. We'd all slipped into acceptance. We'd played Tiddly Winks, Snap Dragon, which ensured Franco singed his eyebrows (a stupidly dangerous game of flaming brandy while trying to scoop raisins from the flammable liquid), Twenty Questions, and the mind-taxing memory game called Elephant Foot Umbrella Stand.

"How about Blind Man's Bluff?" He held up a card.

"What's that?" Tess asked.

"Exactly what it says. Someone has to be blindfolded."

My curiosity piqued at the mention of a blindfold. Anything to do with the resemblance of kink always earned my utmost attention.

Reading the instructions, Frederick replied, "One of us is blindfolded and spun around. The rest of us fan out around the room and take turns to 'bluff' push gently—according to the guidelines—the blind man or woman until they can find said victims and catch them. Then they become the blind man and so on."

"So how do you win?" I ran my thumb around the top of my glass. The game sounded interesting. And thoughts of using a different type of blindfold made my heart hammer. My cock overrode the heaviness of liquor as I became more and more aware of Tess pressed against me.

"Umm." Frederick flipped the card. "Another version is if

the person gets tagged, the blindfolded wearer must correctly figure out who they caught and then they're out of the game." His eyes danced around the room. "It does say to play where there are no obstructions so no accidents occur. Perhaps we should—"

"Here is fine." I stood. The sooner this was over, the sooner I could get Tess into my bed. I had other ideas for a blindfold once we were no longer in company. Turning to my wife, I smirked, "I nominate you, *esclave*."

"Me?" Her eyebrows shot to her hairline. "Why me?"

"Because you've avoided being the centre of attention most of the night. This is the last game, and all of this was your idea. You're up." Hauling her from the chair by her wrist, I manhandled her away from the circle of love-seats. The room was large with open archways and sideboards uniform and neat against the wall. The only things she could trip over were the wingbacks and coffee table.

I could move silently enough that I could keep pace with her, and she'd never know I was there. I'd prevent any accidents.

Franco opened the small box on the table and pulled out a red silk blindfold. Black ribbons dangled on either side ready to secure.

I cleared my throat as my cock grew thicker.

Fuck.

The need to have Tess boiled my blood as the beast inside salivated.

Taking it from him, I ordered, "Turn around, Tess."

Pouting but giggling at Angelique and Suzette, Tess obeyed.

I placed the blindfold over her eyes and tied it tight. Waving my hand in front of her face, I asked, "Can you see?"

Her head tipped up, doing her best to see down her nose at the small sliver of light. Finally, she shook her head. "No. Unfortunately."

I chuckled. "Like old times then."

She licked her lips, thickening my cock even more.

Christ, I needed her out of public and very fucking soon.

She was a drop-dead gorgeous woman. But something was so goddamn sexy about her sight being taken away. I had the ability to do anything I wanted, and she wouldn't see it coming.

My hands landed on her shoulders, slipping over the gold silk of her dress as I spun her around twice. "Spread out." I glared at my fellow players.

Stifling their drunken laughter, they tiptoed apart, moving around the space.

Letting Tess go, I stepped back. "You're free. Go seek."

Her hands came up as she shuffled forward.

No one said a thing as she moved slowly. She came within a whisker of touching Frederick as he glided out of her way.

My palm itched to take out my cock and stroke while watching her move around. I wanted to tear off her dress piece by piece until she was naked with just the blindfold.

I'd sneak behind her and bite her neck, forcing her over the love-seat where we'd snuggled.

Swallowing my groan, my heart bucked out of control as Tess shuffled further around the castle.

It'd only been a few moments since I'd touched her but it felt like an eternity. My fingers missed her. My mouth craved her. And my body….Christ, that trembled with the urge to snatch her from this room and carry her upstairs.

Come on, Tess.

Dépêchez-toi. Hurry up.

This game could go on for hours and my patience was non-existent. Holding my breath, I inched forward and placed my hand behind Suzette.

And waited.

I waited until Tess stumbled past before shoving Suzette forward.

"Hey!" She barrelled into Tess, technically doing what the rules stated and 'bluffed' my blind wife.

Instead of tripping forward, Tess fought the pressure and

spun around, grasping onto her assailant.

For a second, I worried this would bring back bad memories. Memories of monsters and maladies. However, as her hands came up and cupped Suzette's face, she rested her forehead on her friend's. "Gotcha. You're out, Suzette."

One down…three to go.

"Damn it." The woman smiled, drifting off to sit down in a bushel of blue and silver lace. Franco followed his lover with his gaze, swallowing the final sip of his wine. He was so preoccupied with Suzette, he didn't hear Tess as she whispered across the carpet with her arms outstretched and bumped into him.

Make that two to go.

My cock turned to marble.

"Ah-ha!" Instantly, her arms went around his waist, squeezing tight. Her fingers explored his chest with questing curiosity.

A small part of me was jealous. A large part of me wanted to rip her off him and drag her into the dark. But I controlled my urges and relaxed as she reached his chin and announced, "You're out, Franco."

"Fuck." He chuckled, pecking her on the cheek. "So much for lasting the longest." He drifted off to Suzette. Grabbing her hand, he waved at those of us who could see. Pointing at the ceiling, he mimicked going to sleep.

I didn't believe he had any intention of sleeping straightaway, but I let them retire with a curt nod.

The room grew quiet and heavy as they vanished. Tess circumnavigated slowly, searching for her next victim.

Come this way, esclave. *I'll teach you what happens when you find me in the dark.*

Frederick and Angelique managed to stay out of her way, smothering their laughter and daring each other to dash forward and push my wife.

I slouched against the wall, finishing my whiskey and rearranging my erection as Tess moved so beautifully.

Again and again, Tess was bluffed, unable to catch the two trouble makers. My CEO and his wife turned into sniggering children with far too much booze in their blood.

The game could go on all night, and she would never catch them.

That's not going to fucking happen.

I wanted her. I needed her.

I wouldn't wait any longer.

Moving forward silently, I tapped my best friend on his shoulder.

Frederick met my eyes with a question.

Cocking my head at the exit, I mouthed, "Leave. See you in the morning." Pointing at Angelique, I whispered, "Take her with you."

For a second, he looked as if he'd refuse. Then a knowing smirk twisted his lips.

Nodding once, Frederick carefully padded past Tess with her fumbling steps and wrapped Angelique in a hug. Together, they tiptoed from the fire-warmed room leaving Tess smiling and doing her best to navigate the foreign space.

The moment they'd left, I let my inhibitions free; I loosened the bars on my cage and grabbed my hard cock, basking in the knowledge I had Tess exactly where I wanted her.

I could tire her out by following her and never letting her hear me.

I could stalk her. Push her. Slam her against the wall and fuck her.

But I wouldn't.

Because I wanted to tease her first.

Depositing my empty whiskey glass on the sideboard, I moved. Holding my breath, whispering with silence as I'd done for so many years, I reached out and pushed between her shoulder blades.

My skin sparked from touching her.

My stomach clenched with desire to take her.

She was blindfolded but not bound.

I'd rectify that before the night was through.

She stumbled forward with a laugh. "All right, who did that?" Spinning, her arms flailed, doing their best to catch me.

I parried backward, keeping my feet light.

She didn't succeed in touching me, only the wind left in my wake.

Her lips pursed as she tottered forward, searching for my cage. "Q?"

Come to me, pretty Tess.

My heart pounded as I prowled around the room and came up behind her again.

And pushed.

You're mine.

This time, she didn't yield, forcing herself into the push and spinning fast.

A bit too fast.

I jumped back silently; a little closer to being caught.

Well played, wife.

I'd have to punish her for that.

Leaving her alone on the carpet for a few minutes, I followed as she gave up waiting for me to push her again and moved forward gingerly. Holding my breath, I slinked behind her, hand outstretched.

With nimble fingers, I grabbed the zipper on her spine. The dress she wore clung to her skin, but I slid the metal teeth down and down, so gentle and light, she didn't feel the change in pressure.

Her snowy skin revealed inch by inch.

My lungs burned to breathe, and my cock strained against my own zipper to go to her. Be with her. Claim her right on the fucking hearth in this vast unknown castle.

Straightening her shoulders, Tess drifted on.

I moved with her.

My fingers never let go of the zipper, turning her dress from full garment into quickly fanning pieces of material.

Another few steps before the zip reached the base of her spine.

The neckline gaped.

Tess slammed to a stop, her hands flying up, finally feeling the loosening. With a gasp, she was forced to catch the soft dress as it gave up trying to stay upright.

"What on earth?" Reaching behind her with one hand, she found the half-undone garment.

I stepped back, smothering my grin.

Her voice was taut. "Who did that?"

I stayed silent, gritting my teeth at the swell of her just visible ass as the dress sighed around her arms. Her breasts peeked above the neckline, but her embrace kept her decency covered.

I loved the fucking tease of her body.

But I wanted her naked.

I wanted her panting and wet and begging.

I wanted my scissors so I could slice off every last shred of material and touch every inch that was mine.

Tess did her best to refasten the zipper, but it wasn't a one person job. Quickly giving up, she huffed with frustration and dawdled forward. One arm clutched her modesty while the other stayed outstretched as a buffer for any obstacles.

Silly *esclave*.

The only obstacle I'd let her run into was me.

And nothing could save her once that happened.

She looked so sexy, so innocent. Her naked back so creamy and virginal for a whipping.

A growl percolated in my chest.

I bit my lip to stop from making a sound. Once again, I stalked her, letting her walk right past me as I found what I wanted on the sideboard.

A pair of scissors.

I didn't know what they were used for; the blades were tarnished and dull. But they'd do.

Creeping toward her again, I snipped a small hole in the

side of her dress, running the sharp metal with a quick slice around her waistline.

She stiffened and whipped to the side.

I ducked beneath her arm, continuing the slice around her torso to the zipper at the back. With a final snip, the silky material separated from the half-undone bodice and cascaded to the floor.

"Oh, no—" Tess scrambled to keep her dress from fluttering into ruin, but she had to make a choice: let her braless chest be on display or fumble at the bottom where her garter belt and beige tights complimented the white knickers that left nothing to the imagination.

This time, I couldn't hold back my groan.

The staff had gone to bed.

Our friends had vanished at my bequest.

We were alone.

But it didn't mean the castle didn't have eyes in the walls and ears in the curtains.

I wanted to fuck my wife.

But I wanted to do it privately.

Stalking the small distance between us, I scooped her from the carpet and slung her over my shoulder. "Enough."

"Q, wait—" She squirmed in my arms, her tiny fists on my lower back. "How did you move so soundlessly? I'll never get used to it."

I smiled ruefully. "The ability not to be heard comes in handy in most things." I pinched her ass. "For parlor games and other reasons." My trousers tented with my rock-hard erection. "I like watching you without you knowing I'm there."

She trembled, prickling with energy.

My skin electrified with the thought of having her all to myself.

Just like I'd never played innocently with friends, I'd never played like this before.

Ruthless but loving.

Rough but fair.

My wife.

My equal.

I'd missed out on love and company in my life but now had so much more than I fucking deserved.

A small cry escaped her lips as I carted her from the great hall. "What are you doing?"

"Claiming my prize."

"Your prize?"

I bit her hipbone, sinking sharp teeth into feminine flesh. "You."

She shuddered in my arms, flinching a little as I bit too hard. "Did you have to ruin my gown?"

"That gown was hiding what I needed to see."

"Damn you, Q. I loved that dress."

I spanked her ass. "And I love you."

"Strange way of showing it. You wouldn't have destroyed it if you'd known how much it cost."

I chuckled. "You should know by now I don't care about things like cost and expense."

She pinched my lower back. "Well, you should."

"Why?"

"Because you have to decide what I'm worth to you one day."

Shaking my head, I took the castle steps two at a time and barged into our bedroom. Placing her on her feet, I shed any resemblance of a man and smiled with masked serenity and rabid severity.

My fingers shook as I undid the bow of her blindfold, returning her vision.

She blinked, lips parting.

"Oh, *esclave*. When will you understand? Nothing else matters and you could never be assigned a monetary figure."

She breathed heavily as I wrapped my hand around her neck and slammed her against the wall. Her eyes darkened, pupils dilated, and her ruined dress shrugged off within seconds. "Why?"

"Because you, my dear wife, are absolutely fucking priceless."

Tess

THE NEXT DAY didn't begin until noon.

After our drinking games and then Q's wickedness and my multiple orgasms, we were slow getting out of bed.

When we finally did convene in the great hall for a full English breakfast and catch up on emails and conversation, we laughed and smiled with an air of holiday relaxation with all the time in the world.

It'd been so long since I'd been completely carefree— since I'd seen Q so…serene.

Organising this against his wishes had been a risk. I'd been worried sick about telling him. But it had paid off.

Hopefully, the rest of the weekend will go as well.

While the men took care of a little correspondence and business, the girls and I grabbed a few parasols and magazines and headed outside to the large sweeping gardens hidden behind stone walls.

For winter, the weather was kind. The sun shone bright and fierce, doing its best to hide the icy chill and encourage us to indulge in its brightness.

Claiming three of the six blue and white loungers already fluffed and prepared for us, we spent a wonderful few hours reading, sunning, and sipping on virgin daiquiris before we were joined (or more like interrupted) by our men.

Tomorrow was Q's birthday, and today, I hadn't planned a thing. I didn't want to cram events and schedules into this getaway. That wasn't what it was about. This was about unwinding and remembering how nice it was not to have anything to do.

The men took the free loungers, and instead of demanding we go for a walk or head to the river below to fish, they all dozed in the sunshine.

Even Suzette and Angelique nodded off while I watched my family and thanked the universe for everything I'd been given.

Lunch was served outside. Delivered by the attentive servants and placed on convenient side tables at the perfect height for our loungers.

Q chewed the rustic bread and duck pâté slowly, his French voice punctuating the cool afternoon as we shared harmonious company. "Good choice, Tess. This…it's perfect."

My skin shivered with delight that I'd been able to coerce and impress him.

He caught my eye, dragging me back to memories of last night and what he'd done. How he'd held me against the wall and stripped me. How he'd used the thick cord from the velvet curtains to truss my ankles to my wrists, keeping me wide and at his mercy. How he'd made me beg and taken his time after the quick session we'd had in the barn—making up for it with the luxury of pleas and commands.

By the time he'd finished with me, my ass was red from his palm, and multiple pleasure had melted my insides.

Q smiled, following my train of thought.

Flushing, I looked away, finishing my lunch before he could entice me back into his lair and ruin any hope of spending the rest of the day with friends. He was such a master of control. He kept my mind purely on him and our physical want for each other. The intensity between us didn't give me space to worry about what he was hiding.

He has a few more days to tell me.

I just had to hope he kept his promise.

Once we'd devoured our lunch with crisp grapes and decadent cheese, we unanimously agreed a walk would be good now the sun had disappeared behind greyish clouds.

Even in winter, France was a heavenly vacation spot. We couldn't sunbake in bikinis, but a jumper and jeans kept us perfectly warm. However, as we retreated inside to don walking shoes, jackets, and hats, we knew by the time we returned from our stroll, it would be glove and fire weather.

As we struck off two by two, I clasped Q's hand and fell even more in love than I already was. Everything was going so well. Now, if only I could get him to tell me what was bothering him, everything would be perfect.

* * * * *

"I want to do something."

I looked up from brushing my hair and getting ready for bed. "Do what?"

After our walk, we'd all opted for a light dinner of cold cuts and Eaton mess dessert before retiring to our separate quarters. Being outside all day had drained us, and I needed everyone to be energetic for tomorrow.

"I've been thinking about it for a while. I even brought the gear with me…on the off chance you'd agree."

Placing my hairbrush on the marble countertop by the sink, I turned to face him. "Agree to what?"

His nostrils flared as he stormed from the bathroom, heading toward the fireplace. "Fuck, don't worry about it. I've already asked so much of you. It's pointless after you've branded and marked yourself as mine."

Scurrying across our castle bedroom with its old world mystique and history, my white negligee fluttered like wings around my legs. Goosebumps darted over my skin—partly from the cold, but mostly from Q's hesitation. I wanted to wrap myself in the dressing gown spread out in preparation on the bed. But I didn't pause. I went straight to Q.

Flames popped and crackled, spewing furnace heat. However, even with the roaring fire, the room was nowhere near as warm as our home.

Placing my hand on his tense forearm, I said, "No, you

don't get to do that. Yes, I've done those things. But I'm always open to more. I want to know. Tell me what you want to do. And while you're at it, tell me what else you're keeping secret."

He glowered, breaking my hold on him. Pacing toward the window, he breathed hard. Condensation formed on the icy pane of glass. "You're so demanding."

"And you wouldn't have it any other way." I crossed my arms. "Now, tell me."

Not glancing at me, he murmured, "It would mean pain, but well below your threshold."

He deliberately ignored my attempt at finding out what he hid, focusing on the present worry.

Fine, I can be patient…I think.

"Have I ever given reason to hint that I'd say no to you?"

"No, and that's maybe the point." Dragging a hand through his hair, he turned to face me. "Don't you think there should be more limits between us?"

"Limits?" My eyes shot wide. "What do you mean?" Once again, the fear that Q no longer wanted the kinky, violent world we indulged in slithered around my heart.

He said I'd kept him sick. That if I were any other girl who didn't get off on pain, he would've found a way to fix himself and kill whatever monstrous urges tormented him.

But if I were a girl who ran from handcuffs and screamed at the sight of a whip, then Q would never have seen me. He would never have noticed my strength and will to fight him. We would never have given into each other or got married or shared so many years having fun and experimenting with all sorts of wondrously sexual things.

My heart ached. I rubbed at the spot on my chest. "Q—"

His hand slashed through the air. "Forget it, Tess. I'm not ready to talk about that." Planting his stance wide, he growled, "Let's stick to the matter at hand. I want to do this. It makes no sense. But I want to. Would you agree to it without knowing what it is?"

Q often did this.

Tested my willingness. Confident (until recently) in my steadfastness of never denying him. I'd only ever used the safe word once, and that was because he emotionally hurt me rather than physically. And the moment I'd said it, I wanted to take it back.

In fact, if it hadn't been for Frederick helping snap Q out of it, and for Q giving himself up as the ultimate sacrifice to break my depression, I doubted we would be in such marital bliss. I would've walked out of his life and most likely ended up in a psychiatrist's office for the rest of my days doing my best to get past it.

He didn't understand how much I valued him for that. How much I hated myself for the silver scars I'd laced upon his face and chest when I lost myself to rage and whipped him.

I'd tied him to the bed and hurt him.

All in the name of returning to him.

If he could face his worst nightmare and permit me to almost kill him, then anything he asked of me was trivial. I would never hesitate. "Yes, I would. No question. Whatever you want, I accept. However, the moment it's done, I want to know what you're keeping from me. Promise."

His eyes shadowed. "I still have a few days—"

"Promise, *maître*, or…no deal."

Dangerous, deafening silence fell between us. His head lowered, watching me from his darkened brow. "You'd say no to me?"

I was so in-tune with my husband—so used to his ferocity and inner demons that I *felt* them clawing at his control. I felt him struggling to accept my demands without punishing me for standing up to him.

Which was contradictory because this entire duel, I believed Q wanted me to disagree. To say no. He pushed and pulled. Wanting me to give in but secretly begging me not to.

What is going on inside his head?

Was he ill?

Was his business doing okay?

Were *we* okay?

What if he wanted a divorce?

My chest ached harder. What if he'd wanted to tell me for months but I'd arranged a stupid birthday celebration and made it impossible for him to deliver the truth?

Tears burned my vision even as I laughed at what a preposterous idea that was.

Q and I…we were fated. Custom created and thrown together by a world that tried to destroy us.

He wouldn't toss me away.

He couldn't.

He needed me just as much as I needed him.

Q stiffened as my thoughts completed their terrifying circle and settled back into acceptance of my place and the rock solid foundation of my marriage.

I wouldn't be that woman who doubted and became contrary with her convictions. He was mine. Forever.

Whatever it was Q kept secret, it wouldn't break us. That knowledge alone gave me the strength to not push and give him time.

Drifting forward, I held out my hand, cursing the slight tremble. I had the strangest urge to shake on our agreement even though he'd given me no such oath that he'd tell me what was bothering him.

Prowling toward me, Q ignored my outstretched hand and cupped my cheek. "Don't ever doubt me, Tess. Never doubt us."

My eyes locked on his mouth. "I know. And I don't."

He gave me a look as if to say he'd heard my previous thoughts, tasted my fleeting fear.

I dropped my gaze. "I had a second of weakness. That's all. I love you, Q. If you need time…time is what I'll give you. Along with whatever else you want me to do."

His lips landed on my forehead in the sweetest sin-filled kiss. "I'm so glad to hear that, *esclave*."

My nipples pebbled as he gathered me close, nipping at my

earlobe. "Now go to the bedroom down the hall. Last on the left. It's the prettiest I could find on this level." His nose nuzzled my throat, making me listen with my heart rather than my ears. "I'll be there soon. Take this and obey each instruction."

His command made me wet and eager. My fingers curled around a small piece of paper as he tucked it into my hand.

The moment I'd accepted the page, he let me go and vanished out the door.

1. SILK BLINDFOLD (FROM the game last night)
2. Flogger
3. Needle
4. Black ink (all courtesy of my luggage)
5. 1934 Pol Roger Brut Champagne (thanks to *Castelnaud-des-Fleurs*)
6. And a present for Tess that I planned on using many nights to come (she hadn't been the only one buying gifts secretly)

Thirty minutes after Tess left, I stalked through our temporary home and mentally ticked off the list, ensuring I had everything I required. The black satchel in my hand—that'd been hidden at the bottom of my suitcase—clinked softly with what I intended to do to Tess. What she would let me do because she was mine and tomorrow was my birthday.

I planned to spend all night and most of the early morning indulging in her.

What better way to grow a year older than spending it balls deep in my wife?

Tess knew I didn't do puppies and petals. But that didn't mean I wasn't up to celebrating a night dedicated to love and connection.

By fucking her.

By marking her.

By letting my beast out to play and escorting Tess into the darkness she coveted and came alive in. My little sparrow was the kinkiest plaything imaginable, and the moment I let myself off my tightly controlled leash, she met me bite for bite.

Tonight would be no different.

Only…maybe it should?

That damn thought tormented me again. For months, I hadn't been able to run from such conclusions. I'd always been a firm believer in doing whatever felt natural. But what if this *wasn't* natural? What if I was stopping Tess from other experiences by keeping her chained to my demonous urges?

Either way, tonight wasn't a night for reform.

My bare feet padded on the thick burgundy carpet as I passed empty rooms of our rented castle. How many other couples had indulged in fucking and degradation and every morbid, twisted delicious thing Tess and I did within these walls?

Were we the wildest or the tamest compared to the ancestors who'd once roamed here?

My cock hardened with every step. My lips smirked, thinking of Tess and my instructions.

I had no doubt she would've obeyed. Not because I commanded her but because she loved it. She submitted because she wanted what I did. She let me do nasty things to her because she enjoyed it just as much as me. My dirty wife begged for things that would terrify vanilla loving girls.

She wasn't a princess.

Fuck no, Tess was my queen. My sinning, cursing, fucking twisted queen.

She still believed I held the cards in our marriage, but she couldn't be more wrong. I'd barely managed to stop from taking her in our bedroom half an hour ago when she looked at me as if I caused her pain. Pain I could stop if only I were honest with her.

I wanted her.

No, I was beyond that. I was fucking obsessed with her. She was more than my world. She was more than my lover, best friend, and partner. She was the blood in my heart, the breath in my lungs, the fucking marrow in my bones. Without her, I wouldn't exist. Without her, my body would be nothingness: no heartbeats, no mind, no man...no animal.

Cutting off my thoughts, I refocused.

The instructions I'd given her came back to mind.

Dear Esclave,

If you wish to please me, you will do the following. Do not dally or disobey. Do not touch yourself or do anything to displease me. Obey me, my dear Tess, and I will reward you.

1. Shave your pussy until it's bare and dripping

2. Tie up your hair in plaited pigtails

3. Dress in the provided blood-red lingerie you'll find in the room

4. Then wait

5. And Tess...make sure your brand—the very one I marked you with—is visible and glowing with my possession

I'm coming for you.

Your Maître.

My breathing slowed as I stopped outside the room where she waited.

My bag brushed against my trouser leg, whispering with sinful promise. My hands shook slightly—not from fear but monstrous anticipation.

I wanted my wife.

I needed my *esclave*.

I loved them both.

Twisting the handle, I entered the room.

The most beautiful scene welcomed me. Tess had gone one step further. She'd swept up her hair, dressed in the sexy lingerie, and attached the diamond collar with a tag marking her as mine. The brand was covered, but the collar did the same thing—letting me know she was totally under my control.

I didn't know she brought that here.

The collar had been an anniversary gift two years ago.

Her grey-blue eyes glanced my way. Blonde hair cascaded over one, catching on her black eyelashes. She'd done what I asked and plaited the long length into two messy pigtails. However, soft tendrils escaped the imprisonment.

My cock punched my belt.

I dropped my bag.

I love you, Tess. And I'll tell you what I'm lying about. Soon.

"You obeyed me."

Her head bowed, her legs spreading wider, revealing the gift I worshiped daily between her legs. "I did. I look forward to my reward."

My lips curled; the darkness enveloped me. The beast inside stretched, unsheathing its claws, lengthening its spine in preparation.

I stalked toward her and fisted her hair. I fell more in love than I already was.

This woman made me come alive. This woman would end up killing me. But my life was already hers, and I would die gratefully on the pyre of her affection.

"Tu connaiss les règles, esclave." You know the rules.

"What rules, *maître?*"

"You don't get your reward until you've been punished."

Her gaze glittered with rebellion and retaliation but not one ounce of fear—the perfect cocktail for a bastard like me. "Go ahead. You'll never break me."

"Ah, my sweet, sweet Tess. That might be the case…" I nipped at her bottom lip. *"Mais ça ne m'empêchera pas d'essayer."* But it won't stop me from trying.

Dropping the black bag by her spread legs, I tugged on her right plait. "Up."

Unfolding immediately, she stood quivering before me.

Her chest rose and fell, imprisoned in the dark red bra I'd handpicked for her. Her flat stomach shadowed with faint bruises from previous nights, and I traced the bite mark I'd left on her hipbone after our parlour games.

I wanted to do what I'd planned now. To get it over with before she could have second thoughts. But I restrained myself. Anticipation would make it that much sweeter.

Gripping her jaw, I kissed her with a wet-as-fuck dominating kiss before pushing her backward to the bed.

She obeyed every prompt. Falling onto the bedspread, she watched me with desire-glittering eyes.

This room was very much like our assigned accommodation, only smaller. The fireplace roared with heat and the four-poster bed hung with midnight blue drapery rather than forest green.

My jeans and t-shirt became too tight as my body prepared to tease and torture.

Tess squirmed on the mattress as I moved toward her and yanked her up the bed by her arms. The moment she was in the middle, I uncoiled a piece of Japanese silk rope from my pocket and looped it around her wrist.

With a sharp smile, I secured her to one of the four bedposts.

It was a risk tying her down like this. After all, she'd done the same to me when I'd given her my nightmares to hopefully break hers. However, no memory of that day hovered in her gaze. Her skin already flushed with lust as I fastened her other wrist and moved toward her ankles.

She didn't speak—she was too well trained—but her eyes never left my ministrations.

She gasped as my fingers ran around her ankle, cupping her heel protectively before wrenching her legs apart and securing them as tight as her wrists.

Once finished, she lay spread-eagled with no hope of escape.

I stood and surveyed my fucking delicious woman. The

lingerie barely hid her bare pussy, shadowing it in red lace while her bra couldn't hide the pinpricks of nipples begging me to bite.

Running a fingertip from her instep to her clit, I murmured, "So pretty and no chance of running. What shall I do with you?"

Her hands fisted, her lips parting with breath. "Anything...do anything you want."

"Anything?" My fingers pinched her pussy, indenting her soft flesh with the lace protecting her.

She gasped, white cheeks flushing so prettily. The scrap of material couldn't hide how wet and hot she was, drenching the delicate underwear.

Her desire matched mine.

I was rock-fucking-hard for her.

"I'll give you a choice, Tess." Rubbing her pussy, I pressed hard and swift. "Pain or pleasure first? You make the call."

Her back bowed as I stabbed at her entrance, prevented from entering her by the lacy garment. Soon, that bastard chastity belt would be sliced away. But for now, it kept me focused. Gave me a barrier I wasn't permitted to break.

Her eyes switched from dove-grey to dark blizzard. "Pain...I pick pain first."

I shook my head, stealing my hand from her core and bending to unzip my black bag. "Wrong choice."

"But you said—"

I smirked as I kept what I'd pulled from the duffel hidden and prowled to a wall socket by the bedside table. Luckily, the cord was long enough.

We hadn't played with this toy before. But I'd heard good things.

Once attached to the electric source, I kept the device behind my back and repositioned myself between my wife's spread legs.

"I know what I said. But I'm the master here. Not you. And I've decided to give you pleasure first." I bared my teeth.

"Or at least…the hint of pleasure before I hurt you."

Her ribcage stood in stark relief as she sucked in a harsh breath.

She didn't ask questions or demand to know what I had planned because she knew me too well. I wouldn't answer. I'd only show her.

My fingers tightened on the gift behind my back. "Do you know what this is, *esclave?*"

She shook her head. "No."

No? That was surprising. She'd told me about her dildo collection back when she was with Brax. Her battery-operated friends were the only things delivering an orgasm while she wasted her talent on a loveless wonder who believed kissing should be done with the lights off and clothes firmly tucked tight.

He didn't know this woman at all.

But I did.

I knew her sometimes better than I knew myself.

Caressing the large contraption with a soft bulbous end and flexible neck, I switched it on. A loud humming filled the space. Holding it up for Tess to notice, I smirked. "I believe it's called a magic wand."

Her eyes grew round as I cranked up the speed. The tingle of hypnotic vibration shot down my hand.

Interesting.

Experimenting, I placed the end against my cock through my jeans.

"Fuck!" Instantly, I wrenched it away, doubling over with the overload of intensity from the mere touch. Echoes of vicious need radiated down my legs and into my belly.

Tess bit her lip, fascinated and imploring.

I chuckled as I rested my knees on the bedspread. "Oh, I think you're going to like this."

She nodded; her face glazed and sex-soaked. I hadn't even touched her yet, but she'd panted herself into subspace.

Hovering the vibrating wand over her body, I tortured her

a little by pressing it against her ribcage, hipbone, and upper thigh. Anywhere and everywhere but the one place she desperately craved.

Each time I touched her, a moan fell from her lips. Her legs writhed and her fingernails dug sharply into red-flushed palms.

"Do you want this?"

"Uh-huh…" Her eyes rolled as I carefully swiped over her pubic bone.

"How much?"

Her voice strangled. "*So* much."

"Will you fight for it?"

Her eyes opened, struggling to keep me in focus. "Fight?"

"Will you beg for it?"

A calculating gleam entered her gaze. "Do you *want* me to beg for it?"

My cock lurched as she licked her lips.

Her face tensed. "The day you accepted me, I promised I'd fight you, Q. For years, I've never given you complete control over me. You have limits, but you don't trust yourself not to cross them." Her eyes drifted down my front to my erection stabbing at my belt. "However, I give all of that up. Right now. I won't fight. I won't argue. I'll let you do anything you damn well please. Just let me come so I can focus on the rest of the night without going out of my mind."

I leaned over her, hovering the wand over her pussy. "You're going out of your mind?" The low setting hummed with promise. I wanted to see how fast this would make her climb. How quick she could come before I denied such a release.

"Every time you bind me and tease me, I go out of my mind."

I smiled. "I love your honesty. How about one more truth?"

She stiffened, her hips rocking subtly. "Anything."

"Tell me why I do this. What do I want from you?"

She paused, breathing hard. "Everything."

I shuddered. She was so damn right. I did want everything. And for years, I thought I had everything. But now…now, I was missing something. *We* were missing something. And I wanted to find it with her.

My heart raced like a demonic creature, bucking for touch and taste and togetherness.

"You earned this, Tess." Pressing the wand against her clit, I held it there.

Immediately, she let out a ragged groan. Her hips rose to force her flesh harder against the unforgiving vibration. "Yes…oh, *God*. Yes."

"Let yourself go. Let yourself fly. I want to watch you come undone."

Her head thrashed to the side as her forehead knitted together. "I'll do whatever you want."

Whatever I want?

That offer came with no caveats or conditions.

It should.

Tess said she hadn't fully given herself to me. She had. She'd given me her ultimate trust. Trust that I didn't deserve, as I wasn't as human as she believed.

"Q…I—I want you." Her hips came up, her limbs fighting the silk rope. Her breathless softness erupted the sexual hunger savaging my insides.

Cranking the speed, I rubbed the wand from clit to entrance over her knickers.

Her head fell back, eyes rolling. "Oh, wow…"

Climbing over the bed, I lay down beside her. My hand ached from holding onto the vibrating device, and the bed rocked as Tess fucked the toy, desperate for a release.

With my free hand, I snatched her cheeks, wrenching her face to mine.

Every part of her from blood to brain was mine. She had no other thoughts but me. No other worries or concerns or questions.

I owned her completely.

And in return, she owned me.

I kissed her.

I captured her mouth like she would vanish. My tongue speared through her swollen lips, and I fucked her with taste and breath.

She moaned, drawing tight against the restraints, craving my mouth, moaning for the wand.

My leg flung over hers, and she trembled beneath me. She was in the sweetest surrender, and I wished I could record it. Tape her freedom and fucking perfection as she chased her orgasm.

Knowing she let me bring her to the precipice of insanity night after night made my soul ignite until flames in my chest matched the flames in the fireplace. Nothing was more satisfying than her affection. Even her utmost submission wasn't as perfect as her vows to love me in sickness and in health.

That was the ultimate aphrodisiac.

My hand rocked, giving her more friction with the wand.

"Yes…yes…oh, yes." Her breathing stopped as it always did as she strained to release. I hovered in indecision. Part of me wanted her to come. To ricochet into pieces and languishly agree to whatever else I requested. But the other part of me didn't want to give pleasure so easily.

She had to earn it.

And she hadn't…not yet.

Pressing the button, the vibrations ceased.

The room fell silent apart from her tattered breaths. "What—no, Q. I was so close. No…you can't stop there." A pretty pout formed on her lips, her eyes bright and glazed with need. *"Please*…pretty, pretty please? You told me to fly. I want to fly, dammit!"

Rolling from the bed, I placed the wand on the quilt and grabbed the small pouch from my bag instead. "You'll get the rest of your reward once we've finished."

"I want it *now*." Her hips surged upward, looking for more torment. "You're evil."

I laughed. "That isn't new information for you."

Her eyes narrowed, falling to the black pouch as I unzipped it. "What's that?" She did her best to raise her head but the weight of not coming drowned her, making her sleepy.

"This is pain, *esclave*. And you promised you'd let me do anything."

A slight groan escaped her, but she nodded. "I did, and I do. Just…hurry so I can come. I really, *really* want to come."

I chuckled as I sat on the edge of the bed and undid the knot around her left wrist. She never took her eyes off me as I opened the bag and placed the tattoo pen with its vial of black ink on the bedspread.

Her eyebrows rose. "Wait. You're going to *tattoo* me?"

I grinned. She wasn't averse to the idea of needles and forever-after ink. Only focusing on the fact that I would be the one inscribing her body.

"Do you have a problem with that?"

I waited, inspecting every fleeting thought on her face.

For a second, she hesitated. "Umm…"

My back whiplashed straight. "*Umm?*"

Tess's eyes grew wider. "Q…I love you, but tattooing me…that's something I have to think about." Her throat tilted, exposing a little of her fire-seared brand beneath her collar. "Isn't this enough?"

I shook my head. "Nothing will ever be enough. Not now that you've taken my last name or wear my mark or sleep beside me every damn night. I'm a fucking insecure bastard when it comes to you, Tess. And because I know I'm asking a lot, I'll even let you go first."

"Me?" she squeaked. "You want *me* to tattoo *you*? Q, I can draw sharp lines and copy a building, but I've never been good at landscape, portrait, or anything other than sterile architecture."

"Good to know. But I'm not asking you to draw on me.

I'm asking you to *write* on me."

"You obviously haven't seen my handwriting."

"As long as it's legible, I don't give a fuck." I pointed at my knuckles. "You can write wherever you want, but I suggest somewhere I can see every day."

Tess's gaze fell to my offered limb. "You want me to write on the back of your hand?" She froze. "You're insane. I'm not coming anywhere near you with something so permanent."

"Not only will it be permanent, but I also requested the darkest ink available. I want it visible. I want it thick and seen."

"It means that much to you?"

"You know me well enough that you don't need an answer to that."

Her reluctance faded as she stared into my eyes. Love replaced reluctance. Her hurry to come tempered. "In that case, I don't want to go first. Go ahead."

"You're not going to ask where I'm going to tattoo you?"

Her eyes dropped to my t-shirt, no doubt seeing my sparrow and storm design beneath the material. "If it's half as beautiful as your art, I don't care."

"I'm not an artist, Tess."

"You are to me."

Not replying, I brought her left hand upward and inserted her ring finger into my mouth.

Her eyes snapped closed as her body leapt on the sheets. The magic wand rested unalive between her spread and bound thighs. "God, Q. You can't do that if you don't want me to come."

My tongue swirled around her finger, tasting salt and orchid-frost that was a scent uniquely Tess. "I can't?" My teeth nipped her fingertip. "Why not? Could you come like this with nothing else?" Keeping her finger in my mouth, I dropped my free hand and cupped her brashly between her legs. "Or do you need this to be fucked in order to release?"

Her body bucked against me. Her finger hooking inside my mouth as if she could wrench me closer and finish the task

I'd started.

My teeth tightened around her wedding ring and diamonds, slowly removing them over her knuckle, thanks to the wetness of my tongue.

She was too focused on my hand on her cunt to pay attention.

Yanking her finger from my mouth and my touch from her pussy, I sat back and spat her rings into my palm. "There…we won't need those for a while."

Tess blinked. "What? Why?" Panic flared. "Don't you want to be married any—"

I slapped a hand over her lips. "Quiet."

Questions burned on her face as I kept her silent. My cock throbbed as thick desire threaded through my blood. Having her stare at me with such longing and passion almost destroyed my plans, demanding I slide inside her.

"Yes, I want to remain married, *esclave*." Letting her mouth go, I murmured, "But rings can come off…just like I've shown."

Her cheeks blanched. "I don't understand."

"You will."

Her eyes flashed with small threat of rivalry. She didn't say a word as I ripped open an antiseptic wipe and smeared it over her ring finger, making sure to wash away my saliva.

Tossing away the finished rag, I grabbed the surgical needle and tore open its sterilized packaging before inserting it into the tattoo gun as I'd been shown. Louis had given me the supplies when I'd popped in to see him last month to update a few feathers on my chest. He'd worked on my torso piece for months. Multiple visits. Long, painful hours while he engraved and coloured my skin with the redemption of my life. Every pinprick of the needle gave me value for the women I'd rescued, fixating my anger onto the fucking cocksuckers who'd stolen them.

Louis had become a friend even though we never spoke about anything beyond trivial things.

Tess whispered, "The last time I was tattooed, I made the choice to add 58 to my wrist. The first time, the trafficker took away my choice with a barcode, and now, you're going to make that choice on your own."

I froze.

Shit, I hadn't thought of it that way. I hadn't asked her permission. Stupidly, I thought she'd find the notion romantic. She'd let me brand her, after all. This was nothing compared to that.

Tess flinched as my eyes fell to the modified barcode and sparrow on her wrist. Compared to Louis's mastery, the artwork was juvenile. One day, I'd have it lasered off, and if she wanted it redrawn, I'd gladly let Louis replicate the design. Then again, the thought of anyone going near her with sharp needles threatened to send me into a blood rage.

No one else was allowed to hurt her.

Only me.

There I went again, taking control of her body and skin. Something that was hers to ink, not mine.

My shoulders fell. "I don't—"

Her free hand clutched my wrist tightly. "No, I want you to. It's a full circle, Q. Don't you see? I was tattooed to find you, tattooed after I lost you, and now, not only do I belong to you and you to me, but you're the one who will do it."

My heart fucking squeezed. "You don't mind my scrawl?"

She smiled. "Your penmanship is impeccable. I wouldn't trust anyone else." Her spread leg pressed against mine in a blatant show of acceptance. "On one condition."

"Name it."

"I get to do the same to you."

A mark for a mark.

A brand for a brand.

I fisted the gun. "That was already part of my terms."

"Oh, right." A devious smirk twisted her lips. "I forgot because some torturer didn't let me come and my brain is broken."

"You behave and I'll let you come. Deal?"

"Deal." She stretched in her bindings. "By all means, *maître*, tattoo away."

I didn't say anything, mentally preparing for the skin graffiti I'd grace her with. I already knew what I'd write. I just hoped I could pull it off so it didn't look like a four-year-old did it.

Tapping the ink vial, I made sure the gun was operational. "Are you ready to become my canvas, *esclave?*"

"Only if you'll let me come once you've finished your needlepoint." Her lips stole into a cheeky smirk. "And then I'll tattoo you. I'm shaking too much to be of use in my current state."

I pinched her. "You know demands will get you more punishment than reward."

She smiled wider. "Perhaps that's what I'm after. *Especially* if it's delivered with that wand you brought."

My eyes narrowed as I spread her hand over my jean-clad thigh. "Anything can be arranged for you."

Sighing into my control, her hair fanned in messy plaits with a blonde halo. Closing her eyes, she took away the pressure and let me focus.

Bending over her finger, I turned on the gun.

It hummed like the magic wand but at a much lower frequency.

Tess kept her eyes closed but whispered, "Why exactly are you doing this?"

"I'm making it permanent."

"We *are* permanent."

"I want to see it."

"See what?"

I pointed at her wedding finger. "Jewelry can come off, Tess. I want a reminder of the truth just for us beneath the gild of diamonds and gold. I want our vows on my body until I'm ash and bone. I want our promise to seep into your blood and taint your soul."

Her eyes fluttered open. "That's already happened. You own me completely. A tattoo won't change that."

"It will."

"How?"

"It will be the final reminder that we belong. Together."

And no matter what our future holds, no matter what we earn and what we lose in our lifetime together, that's all that fucking matters.

Tess tensed, her mouth hanging open as realization hit. "You want to write *Je suis à toi* on my finger." I'm yours.

I smiled. *"Oui."*

Her body melted into the bedding. "Why didn't you say that? I would never have argued. It's perfect."

"You were right to ask questions." Moving her hand into a more comfortable tattooing position, I growled, "Now, no more speaking. I have to concentrate."

Tess bit her lip as the needle collided with her flesh.

She winced as I slowly wrote the scripture around her tiny finger.

It wasn't easy, and some of my lines weren't perfect, but the vow threaded around her digit directly where her wedding ring sat. The black ink glowed against her skin, forever there. However, unless someone looked under her diamond, they'd never know it existed.

Only me and my beast.

Just as it should be.

It only took a few minutes. Her finger bled just a little, and once I'd completed the final swirl, I daubed the artwork with aftercare cream and wrapped her finger in a protective covering.

Letting her go, I stood and placed the apparatus on the bedside table.

She would ink me in return, but she was right. Endorphins and lust ran through both our veins. My hands hadn't been as steady as they should've been. I wanted her. I'd drawn blood enough to sate the heinous lust inside, but I hadn't hurt her enough to add the utmost pinnacle to her pleasure.

The night was full of possibilities.
And it was time to begin.

I COULDN'T STOP looking at my tattoo.

Not when Q unbound my wrist and ankles. Not when he ordered me to stand at the end of the bed and strip. And definitely not when he secured my legs to the four-poster frame while I stood in a wide stance with my hands on the mattress.

The see-through covering over my new inscription protected and smeared his inked promise but the black calligraphy had seeped into my blood and scripted on my heart, too. The black lettering looked like delicate filigree, ready to be hidden, once healed, beneath my glittering wedding ring.

Q's gorgeous cursive had well and truly marked me as his. I felt more like his wife than I ever thought possible and I wanted to create something with him. I wanted to treasure and cherish every single moment we had left together because life was way too damn short.

"Are you ready?" Q purred behind me.

After stripping off my underwear, he'd inspected my bare pussy, ensuring I'd obeyed his commands to shave every inch. It wasn't often he wanted me completely nude, but I understood why tonight.

That magic wand he'd purchased was the devil and God all in one. The softness of the vibrating head against the swollen wetness of my clit had spun me so tight and hot, so fast and strong; I worried that when I did come, it would cleave me in two.

I didn't want to die via orgasm. Especially now Q had written ownership on me with his own hand.

"I asked, are you ready, *esclave*?" He swatted my behind.

He couldn't hide his tremble or erection. The large mirrored wardrobe to my right showed a kinky, erotic scene. Q had stripped, too. He stood with a lambskin flogger in his hand while every inch of him was deliciously naked.

His cock speared in front, just as bare as I was. He'd shaved to match.

I shivered in anticipation of our slick skin sliding and slapping and fucking and taking.

My head lolled as desire made everything so heavy and tender. "Yes. Yes, I'm ready."

"Ten strikes for being such a good wife. If you deserve more afterward, I'll give them to you. But for now...I'll go easy."

I nodded, placing my cheek on the mattress. My fingers curled into the soft sheets, activating the burn of my tattoo.

The first whistle of the flogger reached my ears just before the sharp bite punished my ass.

Q sucked in a harsh breath, growling in his chest. "Count for me, Tess."

"One."

He'd struck me so many times; my body no longer fought the sting. It slipped and liquefied, swirling down and down into the sensual darkness inside my mind. Q could whip me for hours, and I would love every strike because he could hurt my mortal body but not my immortal soul. That latched onto his, making love without boundaries all while our outwardly forms punished each other.

Q raised his arm again.

The flogger lacerated the air, landing on my skin. "Two."

He didn't pause, punishing me quickly.

I shuddered. "Three."

Another. "Four."

And another. "Five."

"Six."

"Seven."

"Eight."

My legs grew weak, and I gave more and more weight to the mattress. My clit throbbed, and if he angled the flogger between my legs, I would come within a splinter of a second.

The whistle came again. "Nine."

And a final time. "Ten."

Q huffed hard as he threw away the whip and fisted the blindfold from last night. His skin blazed while his eyes shot black with monsters. He was so fucking hot. So primal and proud and strong. Sometimes, I deliberately angered him just to see the different pigments of rage upon his skin and hear the different tones of abuse in his voice.

I loved his madness.

I loved our crazy, wonderful life.

Somewhere in the room, the soft chime of midnight heralded Q's birthday.

"Happy birthday, *maître*." Wriggling my ass, I implored. "I think the only way to bring in such a day is to be cock deep in your very willing wife."

Q lashed the blindfold from behind me. Instead of going for my eyes, he looped it around my throat.

He'd asphyxiated me before. He'd taken me to the edge of unconsciousness more times than I could count. Sometimes, instinct bellowed over my trust of him, demanding I scream my safe word.

But I never did.

Because Q, no matter his low thinking of himself, was so much more than just a monster.

He was a lover.

A protector.

A giver and friend.

He was so much.

However, he wants more.

But what?

What more could he give me?

What more could *I* give *him*?

"I agree with your offer, *esclave*." Q's cock wedged against my ass as he tightened the blindfold around my throat. "How much do you want me to fuck you?"

"This much." I bucked backward, standing on my tiptoes to slip up over his erection and position my pussy directly over his crown.

He jolted; the blindfold cut into my windpipe as shock and lust stole him. "Fuck, you're too flexible for your own good."

I arched my hips, forcing the tip of him to enter me.

The room littered with filthy curses from my French master. "Shit, Tess. Having you spread, seeing every inch of you, feeling your wetness while watching my cock disappearing inside your body—your body that's red and welted and marked and tattooed with everything belonging to me—Christ, it makes me want to fucking come all over you."

His body sandwiched mine from behind as his cock shot into me with one swift thrust.

I cried out, but no oxygen got past the blindfold. Softness teased my vision and lack of air made every sensation exquisitely consuming.

My body was so full. Too full. His hips punished mine, pulling out and driving back in.

His tight hold around my neck relaxed a little.

I sucked in a noisy breath.

His weight slipped to the side as he grabbed the magic wand and switched it on.

I moaned loudly, "Q, if you touch me with that—"

Too late.

He positioned the vibrating animal right on my clit just as he thrust deep and hard.

I didn't stand a chance.

The earlier denial of my orgasm. The fear of what would happen when I let go.

None of it mattered.

I screamed.

And came.

My spine bolted into one electric rod of bliss. My inner muscles clenched greedily around him, over and over with mind-deleting pleasure.

I screamed and came for I didn't know how long. My spread legs made the torture all the more painful. The thick control of Q fucking me made my entire body clench and shudder.

He turned the vibrating devil higher, pressing harder against my clit.

"Shit!"Another bomb arced down my spine and detonated through my womb into my legs and toes.

I sobbed as I crashed back to earth. But Q didn't remove the vibrating nemesis.

"Q…please."

"Another, Tess."

"No." I bit the sheets as he angled the device even harder against me. He bruised me both inside and out. Slipping the wand from my clit to my asshole, he held it against us. Torturing his cock as well as me.

"Fuck me. Fuck, fuck, fuck." He bucked harder as the wand turned its magic on the sensitive flesh of his erection.

I rose again, screeching and trembling to another breath-wrenching orgasm.

He grew impossibly harder inside me. One hand held the blindfold around my neck while the other ran the magic wand over us—over his balls, my clit, his cock, my asshole.

I couldn't keep up. I couldn't tell where the head of the machine was and where the echoes of vibrations began. All I could tell was the mattress was soaked beneath my cheek where I panted and drooled and my throat burned for a proper breath.

When Q pressed me deeper into the mattress, sandwiching my pussy against the wand and the end of the bed, I gave up again.

I screamed as every molecule exploded in my extremities.

His voice filled my ears. "Goddammit, *esclave*, you fucking undo me. Feeling you come around me. Knowing I could take your life and you would die right here in my arms because you love me and wouldn't fight. Shit, that's the worst kind of turn-on. The *best* kind of turn-on."

His hips pistoned harder and harder.

I couldn't hold on.

I came again.

And my undoing was his.

With more dirty curses, he followed me, slamming into me. Letting go of the blindfold to hold my hips, he forced me to take every damn inch of his huge size.

By the time we both came down from paradise, I couldn't move.

Literally, I could not move.

It took us ten minutes to find the energy to stand and another ten to untangle the ropes and flop onto our sides to face each other on the bed.

Our breathing remained out of control, and our touches wracked and shook as we stroked and petted, turning violence into tenderness.

Finally, once our jagged, scattered pieces were glued firmly back into order, I murmured, "As much as I want to, I don't think I can tattoo you tonight unless you want words as jittery and unreadable as a baby's."

Q chuckled, gathering me close and spreading me on his naked front. We stuck together with sex-sweat, but I wouldn't have it any other way. "You're excused until tomorrow."

My eyes fell on the champagne bottle on the nightstand. "You brought dessert?"

His smile was wickedly sinful. "Oh, that's for breakfast, *esclave*. We haven't had dessert yet." Spanking my sore ass, he ordered, "On your back, I haven't nearly had my birthday fill of you yet."

"GOOD MORNING, BIRTHDAY boy."

My eyes narrowed at Frederick as Tess and I entered the breakfast hall. *Screw him and his eternal optimism.* I didn't care to be reminded another year had gone by. The life I treasured with my wife and business ventures close to my heart was rapidly running out.

Fuck birthdays.

I didn't reply, glowering at the freshly cooked pastries and berry preserves with toast sitting pretty in a silver rack. Staff milled around, placing plates of scrambled eggs and bacon in the centre of the table.

Frederick laughed at my cold shoulder. "What? Did you wake up deaf as well as a year older, you sullen bastard?"

Tess giggled at my expense.

"That will be the only reference to the date if you value staying in one piece." I pointed a finger at my friend. "Got it?"

Angelique giggled, glancing at Tess and the gingerly way she sat down. "I take it you guys had a good night celebrating?"

Tess blushed, using the excuse to grab a piece of toast to avoid the question. "I don't know what you mean."

Suzette nudged Franco with love hearts in her eyes; at least their own romance kept them from interfering with mine.

Sitting beside Tess, my heart lurched at the black lines from the tattoo peeking beneath her wedding ring. She should've kept the covering on for a few days to heal, but stubborn as always, she'd slipped her rings back on saying she couldn't bear not to wear them. The day I put them on her finger was the day they were glued for eternity.

I loved her sentiment and desire to show the world she was mine—in marriage and harmony. However, I did worry about the healing wound. Later, when we weren't in company, I'd demand she give the ink a few days to heal.

Plus, I'll be able to see my handiwork a little longer before she covers it permanently.

As I ladled a selection of food onto my gold-rimmed plate, the conversation switched to what we would do today. Tess stayed curiously silent as ideas were suggested and tossed away; the concept of boat paddling on the lake discounted in favour of scrolling through the movie channel and hanging out in the castle's converted cinema.

Any suggestion was fine by me. As long as I remained in this bubble of relaxation.

I wouldn't admit it to Tess, but this…it was exactly what I needed. Getting away from work, our house, the constant strain of our companies and charities. I couldn't completely unwind, even here—responding to emails and constantly checking for any meltdowns that needed urgent attention. But the rest of it, I could trust to the legion of employees who hopefully knew how to do their damn job.

The ribbing from earlier was forgotten as we all ate in friendly company. Once our hunger was sated and the sun had risen enough to melt away the frost on the windowpanes, we sat back in drowsy happiness.

Breakfast was cleared away while fresh lattes and macchiatos were delivered.

Tess cupped her steamy caffeine with reverence, inhaling the coffee fragrance.

Sun streamed into the space, highlighting her golden hair, glowing on curls of gold and wheat. Her cheeks pinked with contentedness, and when she caught my eye, she blushed.

Even now…after so many years, she still managed to stab me in the heart and grab my cock with a single glance.

I smiled, falling deeper into her spell, unable to look away. I drank in her dainty fingers around her glass, her lips pursing to blow on the hot froth, and the soft tendrils of hair dancing over her cheeks.

I loved how strong but feminine she was. I loved how innocent but kinky she ran. And I adored how she took nothing for granted. I didn't know if it was her upbringing of being unwanted and ignored, but I surrounded her in decadence and wealth and she didn't covet any of it.

She only cared about me.

Me.

She loves me.

Even after what I'd done to her last night and all the nights of our marriage. No matter how bad I was or the fucked-up things I needed, she accepted me and cherished every part.

I fucking loved her for that.

For so many things.

And I had to be content.

If I couldn't give her what I ultimately wanted…then…so be it.

I had enough to keep me happy until I died.

I would appreciate what I had and not what I didn't.

Tess looked up again, her gaze meeting mine. We shared another soft smile before she looked away and cocked her chin at Suzette, sharing a private, soundless message.

"We'll be right back," she said.

Before I could ask where she was going, Tess and my head housekeeper put down their coffees and vanished from the hall.

Where the fuck are they going?

I glowered at Franco, silently demanding an explanation.

He shrugged. Not giving the game away. However, I didn't think he was as clueless as me—just not willing to ruin whatever surprise the women had in store.

Goddammit. If this was about birthday gifts, I didn't want any.

Tess couldn't buy me anything that I wanted more than her.

Frederick chuckled. "I know that look, Q, and relax. We didn't get you presents. I know how that would go down."

I relaxed a smidgen. But then tensed again as Angelique smirked. "We didn't get you presents. However, it doesn't mean your wife didn't."

Shit, what did Tess do?

Balling my hands, I did my best to control my annoyance. The padding of socked feet met my ears as I spun in my chair as Tess and Suzette wandered back into the room.

I launched upright, staring at what hung adorably in Tess's arms.

Moving shyly toward me, she murmured, "I know you love your birds, Q. And normally, I would've bought you some exotic feathered friend for your aviary. But the last time I was at your office, I saw something that made me pause."

Saw what?

What the fuck did she see to warrant this invasion into our lives?

No one else mattered as my entire attention fell on Tess and the tiny puppy watching me with trusting black eyes. A shaggy version of a French bulldog with an upturned button nose and inquisitive ears never broke eye contact.

Wait…she was in my office. I'd had countless dealings over the past few months. Some I wanted her to know about and others I didn't.

Keeping my voice monotone, I demanded, "What did you see? When you were at work?"

"The shelters."

My jaw tensed. So she had seen that. What about the other charity I'd recently set up?

I stepped slowly toward her, eyeing the mutt.

If she'd seen the animal charity, she might've seen the

others. The paperwork had been side by side until I handed the finalizing to Frederick.

Glancing at my longtime friend and colleague, I raised an eyebrow. I didn't know what I asked Frederick, and I didn't know what his half-shaken head reply meant. Either way, Tess was far too fucking curious for her own good.

Couldn't I have one secret that she wasn't aware of? One hidden desire she didn't need to parade into her light and make me face when I wasn't ready?

Merde! Shit!

Suzette sidestepped me, returning to her place beside Franco. The moment she left, I strode forward and cupped Tess's cheek, doing my best to ignore the wriggling fur ball in her arms. "You didn't have to snoop, *esclave*. Once the organisation was complete, I would've told you."

She smiled, not caring in the slightest I'd kept it from her. Mainly because she knew I spoke the truth. The minute it was a done deal and something I could be proud of rather than worry, I would've told her. I might not have told her about the other charity for some time—giving myself the space to accept what I'd become to suspect—but she had no reason to doubt me. I'd never kept secrets from her...until recently.

"I know, Q. Don't worry about that. I just—I saw the forms on your desk and made a decision. I—I hope you don't mind."

"I don't mind." My hand fell from her cheek, hovering over the soft head of the wriggling black puppy. "However, just because I've donated a considerable sum to animal cruelty prevention and shelters around the world doesn't mean I understand why there's a dog in your arms."

Tess smiled, doting on the small fluff bag. "When I saw the forms, I googled the address of one of the closest shelters. I wanted to see for myself and be a part of it, if you'd let me. When I arrived and asked for a tour, a dog was delivered after being rescued from an abusive asshole."

Her eyes melted into blue sorrow. "Q...the poor thing

was howling and in pain. So afraid. The vet tried to tend to her—give her medicine and show her she'd be cared for, but all I could see when I looked at that poor creature with cuts and bruises and terror in her gaze was me. You rescued me from the same sort of environment. Without you, I could've ended up belonging to some bastard who would've done to me what was done to that poor dog."

She nuzzled her face into the scruff of the animal. "I just couldn't leave her there. The cages at the shelter were fine— she would've had a bed and food and grass to stretch her legs—but Q...I just, I fell in love with her."

Fuck.

The beast inside me rolled onto its back, begging for the same scratch and loving attention Tess doted on the canine. How could I say no to that? How could I ever say no to anything she wanted?

Because she was right.

She could've been any number of unlucky slaves untreasured by devils of the world. It was why I did what I did and hunted rapists and traffickers, rehabilitated victims and abused, and now, extended my reach into the animal kingdom because they were the ones with such a raw fucking deal.

All they wanted was a home and a family.

And a lot of them were either loveless or suffered maltreatment.

I couldn't stand by and let that happen. Neither could Tess. And that made me love her so goddamn much.

I sucked in a breath, my arms aching to grab her in the largest hug. "You did the right thing."

Relief sparked in her eyes. "Really? Oh, thank God." Raising the puppy, she added, "I brought the cutest one...hoping he'd sway you."

My eyes narrowed. "Wait, cutest one? Where's the other dog you mentioned? Why not take the abused one? Puppies will be easier to rehome than an elderly life-broken bitch."

Tess bit her lip, glancing at Suzette across the room. "I,

eh...I did take the mother. I—you have to understand, Q. They're family. I couldn't separate family. How cruel would that be?"

My heart raced, imagining my chateau not only overrun by recovering slaves, but also a first-class kennel to every maltreated animal in France. "What do you mean?"

Tess deliberately broke eye contact, kissing the puppy's wrinkly forehead. "I took the mum and her three puppies. They're at home. I thought it would be best to introduce you one at a time."

What the fuck?

My lips twitched with annoyance and affection. "And what if I'm allergic to dogs or don't want a pack running through my house?"

"Too bad."

"Too *bad*?"

Tess nodded.

My hand itched to spank her for such gall.

"They're ours now. They don't have names yet, but the mum is the sweetest soul, and her pups will grow up to know what it's like to be loved with their family rather than be torn apart and sent to people they don't know."

"They would've found loving homes, Tess." I couldn't tear my eyes away as she sank her fingers into the puppy's fur. Irrational jealousy caught me unaware. I wanted her to pet me. Stroke me. I wanted to be the beast she comforted not some imposter.

But I couldn't help the slight thawing inside as the puppy looked at me, lolling out its tongue in welcome.

Balling my hands, so I didn't reach out and touch the bastard, I snapped, "The animal shelters and charity I've started doesn't condone killing. Each animal is given the best quality of life before their forever home is found."

"Oh, I know. But...Q...I couldn't leave them there. No matter how nice their pen was or the facilities at the shelter. They're babies!"

Baby.

My heart clutched at the word. I couldn't stop my mood from souring or the harshness in my tone. "That's a ridiculous reason."

"It's a perfectly valid reason." Tess passed the pup to me. "Name him, Q. He's yours."

I backed up, wanting nothing to do with something so breakable. I had a hard time keeping Tess safe from myself, let alone a flimsy baby with no sense of fear.

"*Esclave...*"

"No, Q. Hold him." She gave me no choice, shoving the animal into my arms and backing away.

I held my breath as the squirming warm body did something to me that fucking hurt. All my life, I'd run from the notion of family. I never wanted children or weakness by giving my heart to too many people. Tess was the only one allowed to weaken me. If she died, I'd fucking perish with her. That was how deep my love for her went. I didn't want to destroy myself by giving others such a godly power over me.

That wasn't how I worked. I wanted to be strong by being alone. But then Tess came into my life and grabbed the beating organ without any permission from me.

She'd just done it again by giving me a dog that strained its scruffy black neck to lick my chin.

Ah, fuck.

Looking behind me, I focused on Frederick. "Take this. I wish to speak to my wife...alone."

"It's not a this, Q. It's a puppy." Tess scowled. "Give him a name. Any name you want."

"Shut up." I glared at Tess. "We'll finish discussing this later." Holding the dog like a soccer ball under my arm, I marched toward Franco. "Here, take it."

Franco stood quickly, accepting the creature as it yelped with uncertainty. Tess stepped forward, whatever motherly instincts she had raging into gear.

But I held her back, my fingers lacerating her wrist.

"Go. All of you."

The rumble of chairs pushed back and feet sliding over polished floorboards was the only sound as they filed from the hall. Frederick stopped and plucked the puppy from Franco's arms, giving Tess a fleeting grin. "I've got a dog at home. I know how to give a hug. He's safe with me."

Tess gave him a grateful smile.

A flashback of him pulling Tess from my arms when I'd saved her the second time—just before I tore out the heart of the bastard who stole her—added despicable darkness to a sweet scene.

I waited until everyone had left. Staff included.

Once everyone had gone, I stormed toward the large doors and slammed them closed. My eyes darted around the space, searching for another entrance to block.

There was nothing.

As far as I was concerned, we wouldn't be disturbed.

Which was good because depending on how Tess answered my next question, we might need a shit load of privacy.

Tess stood where I'd left her, her eyes never leaving my jerky movements.

Standing with a few metres between us, I kept my fisted hands hidden. "What else did you see, Tess?"

"See?"

"On my desk. In the office. I know there were more forms. Forms you haven't mentioned."

She flinched. "I didn't snoop if that's what you're asking."

"I'm not asking. I know. And I think you understand how it relates to my issue over the last few months."

Her eyes shot wide. "I do?"

Keeping my voice measured, I lowered my brow. "What did you see?"

She backed away a little as I advanced. Her gaze remained on me, not looking where she was going.

"I…I saw another new charity that you've invested

millions into."

"And…"

"And what? I don't know what you want me to say."

"Say what it was."

"The charity?"

I arched my eyebrow. She was playing coy; she knew what happened when she did that. My hand twitched to teach her a lesson. My skin crawled at the dragged out discomfort of such a topic. I hadn't wanted to do this here. But once again, she hadn't given me a choice. Making me face my deepest, darkest desires before I was ready.

I growled, "There was one for the shelters and another for…"

Tess swallowed. "Umm…"

The door clanged open. Angelique darted into the dining room.

Tess and I leapt apart as if we'd been caught doing something wrong.

Doing my best not to roar with frustration, I snapped, "I told you to leave us alone, Angelique."

"I know…I just, Frederick told me—"

The man in question chased after his wife, taking my temper squarely on his shoulders. "I told her I needed to speak with you urgently." Smiling kindly at Tess, he said, "If you go with Angelique, she's arranging the chauffeur to drive us to the local village for a browse. I think it will do us all good to get some fresh air."

Tess glanced my way, her face undecided. She was like me. She hated strung-out arguments and unresolved issues. We needed to talk about this—a lot sooner than I'd wanted but fucking Frederick had ruined the moment.

"What's your deal, *mon ami*?" I snarled. "We need some time. We have no intention of going shopping when this hasn't been discussed—"

Frederick stormed toward me, braving his life to touch my arm. "I think topics such as these should wait until you're at home, don't you?" Lowering his voice, so Tess couldn't hear, he added, "Besides, you're not entirely sure yet. Give it a few more days, Q. Then you can rage all you want."

Fuck.

He had a point.

I still didn't have my head on straight. If I opened this topic with Tess now, who the fuck knew what I would say. I didn't want to hurt her. And the way my anger swirled like hissing dragons in my blood, I just might.

"Fine." My voice was a bite.

Angelique visibly relaxed, looping her arm through Tess's and pulling her from the dining room.

"We're not through with this, Q." Tess fought against Angelique's propulsion "I want to know what you're hiding from me."

Gritting my teeth, I did my utmost to keep my voice neutral. "We'll talk about it when we get home."

"Home or here…it doesn't stop what I saw." Rebellion and fight—the same strength that I made her promise over and over to never let me break—blazed bright in her eyes. "I saw, Q. I know what the other charity was. But you're wrong about me being able to figure out how it attributed to your behaviour the past few months. I said I'd give you time, but you're quickly running out of it."

Shit.

Before I could reply, Angelique gave me an apologetic smile and stole my wife from the room.

Tess

"HE'S NOT VERY good on a lead." I forced my voice to be light and fun-filled but nothing could switch the stagnant air between Q and me. Not even the stumbling puppy currently chewing on his leash by my feet.

Damn Frederick and Angelique for interfering.

If they'd stayed away for just another few seconds, Q would've admitted what he'd been hiding. I was sure of it. He would've had no choice but to spit it out. His temper wouldn't have permitted it any other way.

We would've fought verbally. Hell, maybe even physically, and then we would've made up. We would've spent the entire day in bed, striping each other of our defenses. We would've hurt and healed together.

Instead of this farce.

Why is he so afraid?

Damn man not willing to talk.

I knew him as well as I knew myself, but I wasn't a mind reader.

Suzette and Franco strode ahead, their hands interlocked as they browsed quaint tourist shops and cafes. The cobblestones reminded me of the village where Franco had chased me after I'd escaped and called Brax. But the air of relaxed charm did nothing to tame Q as he stalked beside me.

Frederick did his best to change the mood, chatting quietly

to Q about work matters and things that failed to take his mind off whatever he brooded about.

Angelique gave me more than one smile, holding thousands of questions and no resolutions. Did she have any idea what was going on with my husband? Did Frederick talk to her about whatever Q had said in confidence?

And how damn unfair was it that Frederick knew more about Q's issue than I did?

I'm his wife, dangnamit.

My finger itched beneath my wedding ring, agreeing with that fact. I wanted to wrench off my rings and shove my newly tattooed digit under Q's nose. I wanted to scoop the still unnamed puppy off the street and hit Q over the head with the squirmy tiny body.

Not that I'd ever hurt such a cute creature that way.

I would use much more acceptable devices to punish my husband.

If anyone needed strapping down and hitting, it was him. Purely for driving me mental with worry and confusion.

"He'll get better," Angelique whispered, pacing with me as I left Q to discuss whatever he damn well wanted with Frederick.

Screw him.

If he wasn't man enough to discuss the mess between us, then fine. Two could play the silent treatment. I was aware I'd just contradicted my previous conclusions about giving him time, but there was only so much I could tolerate before I reached a limit.

Not talking was one of those limits.

"Oh, he'll get better all right." I glared at Angelique. "When we get home, he won't have a choice."

My friend patted my shoulder. "It won't be anything you can't overcome together."

Really?

I wasn't so sure. I knew Q. I knew when he sank into his thoughts and twisted himself into hundreds of knots trying to do the right thing. Doing his best at killing himself to be something he wasn't. When he got like that, nothing could reach him. The last time, he'd sent me back to Australia after the best sexual experience of my life.

If he tries to push me away again…

I stopped those thoughts immediately.

I couldn't contemplate that. Anger was much better at keeping the uncertainty and pain at bay. The pain of knowing today was the last day of our stolen vacation, and tomorrow, we'd all travel back to reinsert ourselves into life. And it'd been ruined.

Q would return to work, even though he promised me he'd cut back his hours, and I would continue to be the figurehead for our charities and run the household. He'd use the long hours to keep his issues buried until I blew up at him and we had a fight that rattled the windows of our home.

I glowered at my husband.

Not only had he pissed me off, but he'd also refused to accept his birthday gift.

Well, screw it.

If he didn't want to name this puppy, I would. I wasn't giving him or his siblings and mother up. They needed me. Just like Q needed me even when he pretended he didn't.

My thick winter boots stomped on the cobbles as I announced, "I've thought of what to call the puppy." My gaze fell on the waddling fat form by my ankles. He slipped on the icy ground, pulling this way and that on a leash he had no experience with.

I wanted to pick him up, but he also needed to get used to it.

Everyone's heads snapped toward me.

Q narrowed his eyes, blistering with dark intent. I smiled coldly at him, ignoring everyone else. "I'm going to name him Courage because he actually has the bravery to face scary things in life without tucking tail and running."

Q's face blackened. His body language slipped from

wound up to lithe and lethal.

My muscles trembled; my core automatically grew wet for him. He'd trained me so well that whenever he got the possessive, dominating look in his eyes, it took all my willpower not to bow in the street and beg him to be my master. To hurt me if it made him feel better. To let me hurt him if it made him somehow return to our open, loving relationship.

How had this weekend turned into something so fraught with unspoken barriers?

Frederick grinned. "I get the underlying tones but actually think Courage is a great name. What's the bitch called?"

Ripping my gaze from Q, I focused on Frederick. "Don't call her that. I know it's the technically correct term for a female dog, but she's a mother, after all." Doing my best to make the atmosphere light, after the swirling ferocity between Q and me, I laughed. "Let's not disrespect her."

"Oh, I know." Suzette spun around, walking backward as Franco continued down the footpath to the wrought iron bridge over a babbling brook ahead. "Perhaps Sally? Short for Salvation."

I cocked my head. It could work. We could have a theme of Salvation and Courage and Bravery and Screw You, *Maître,* for being a Wimp.

My heart pounded. "I kinda like it."

Q huffed. "Sally? *Really.*" He rolled his eyes. "First, you bring a pack into my house, and then you name them ridiculous things."

Slamming to a halt, I yanked too harshly on Courage's lead. His fat body flew backward, sprawling by my feet.

Oh, God.

I'd already hurt the poor thing, and I'd only had him a few days.

Keeping him secret since I'd been to the shelter, hadn't been easy. Suzette had kept him in her quarters with Franco at night, and I'd kept the mother and puppies comfortable in the stable by day.

After waving Q and I off in the car at the start of the weekend, Suzette had bundled little Courage with her, and he'd hitched a ride in the helicopter before being looked after by the staff at *Castelnaud-des-Fleurs.*

If Q were so adamant about not having dogs at home, then I would find them new families. But I couldn't deny my heart was already attached. Especially to this little guy.

"It's not a ridiculous name." I planted a hand on my hip, daring Q to take possession of his gift and fall in love like I had. "It fits. And unless you say otherwise, it's sticking."

His nostrils flared. I waited for him to jerk me close and whisper sinful commands into my ear. Instead, he rolled his shoulders, physically forcing himself to relax. The rage siphoned from his gaze, leaving his true thoughts locked to me.

I hated the distance.

The coldness left in his wake as he pulled away.

What was so bad that he couldn't tell me? What was he so afraid of?

I'd stupidly hoped that Q would fall for his animal just like I had. That he would find whatever it was that he'd lost…or perhaps realised he would never have.

Maybe his past had finally caught up with him? The fact he'd dispatched his father, lost his sister and mother, and been alone for most of his days might've damaged him deeper than I knew. Had he not got over that and it tortured him still?

Kissing Courage's head, I dropped my guard and looked at Q with everything bared.

Please…stop these games and talk to me.

I don't like this distance between us.

But he didn't do what I'd hoped.

Instead of tucking me in his powerful embrace and kissing me tenderly, he looked at the picturesque distance and shut me out.

If he wanted to sulk, then so be it.

When he was ready to discuss like a rational person, he would have to grovel.

And I wouldn't make it easy for him.

* * * * *

That night, after our final dinner in the great hall and a few semi-awkward hours drinking by the fire and playing poker, Q and I retired to our room.

The angry standoff from this afternoon had mellowed to a sad chasm, and I didn't know how to cross it.

And Q didn't try.

He had a shower. On his own.

He slipped into his boxer-briefs. Behind closed doors.

He climbed into bed without ordering me onto my knees or any other depraved, delicious thing.

He'd turned inward, and I couldn't reach him.

Even Courage, the French bulldog mix, couldn't touch him. I knew I probably shouldn't (forming bad habits so soon), but with Q's emotional distance and the fear that I'd done something catastrophic with no idea how to fix it, I tucked the puppy into bed with me. I fell asleep holding the snoring black creature all because my husband wasn't available.

My dreams were lost and confused. And for the first time in a long time, I dreamed of Mexico and hallucinations and hurting other women. Q had cured me of so many broken pieces, but the ghostly memories would always be there, waiting to attack me in times of stress.

I woke around three a.m. to an empty bed and galloping heart.

Q was gone.

Courage was gone.

I was alone.

And terrified.

The warehouse and smoking gun from pulling the trigger on Blonde Angel faded as I clutched the bedspread and reminded myself that the nightmare was in the past. That I was safe and loved and wanted.

Only, Q had made me feel the opposite. Tonight, Q had hurt me more than any whip or spur. And I couldn't stomach any more distance between us.

I needed him.

He needed me.

This is stupid.

A simple conversation could clear the air. I was willing to do what was necessary, so why wasn't he? Running my hands over the cold side of his bed, my body craved to slink against his warm form and demand the comfort he'd withheld. I wanted to be touched and rocked to sleep in his masterful embrace. Only then could I find strength to slay my night terrors and be the strong woman Q adored.

Where had he gone? Where had Courage gone?

And why did he leave without a goodbye?

Heart racing, I climbed out of bed and wrapped myself in a fluffy white dressing gown.

Slipping silently from our bedroom, I made my way through the castle, seeking out the two things I needed most.

It took me almost half an hour to find them. They weren't in the great hall or game room. They weren't in the kitchen or many lounges.

When I finally did find them, I huddled against the wall, draped in shadows, not wanting to be seen. Because there, on the frost-bitten grass with the moon wrestling with the dawn, was Q.

Courage stood on two legs, his chubby front feet on Q's knee as he sat on his haunches over the puppy. My lover's breath puffed in icy curls as he scruffed the puppy behind its pert ears.

I couldn't hear what he murmured, but his body said all I needed to know.

Q was hurting.

The master of my heart and owner of my soul was in pain.

And I despite my upset and wish that he would talk, I couldn't remain mad at him.

Instead, I would do everything I could to help.

THE DRIVE HOME was a fucking nightmare.

Courage, the damn puppy, was given prime of place on Tess's lap while I drove the Aston Martin to the brink of its engine capacity. Frederick, Franco, Suzette, and Angelique had returned the same way they'd arrived—in my helicopter—while Tess and I left the large castle behind, following the curved driveway and hitting the patchwork countryside of rural France.

I'd had the good mind to make Tess fly home with them.

I needed some space to get over my fucking self and find peace again. And I couldn't do that with Tess silent beside me.

We hadn't discussed it.

I hadn't been able to sleep, and at some point in the night, the damn puppy needed to piss. Against my wishes, I'd scooped him up and crept through the sleeping castle. I didn't want to be swayed by the animal. I didn't want to fall in love with the breakable body and overly trusting spirit. But in that moment of just man and beast, with frost for company and moon for illumination, I couldn't stop the thawing in my heart.

And with the thawing and affection for another creature came the awful conclusion that what I'd been trying to convince myself I didn't need these past few months was more than just a need. It was past rational sense or understanding. It was deeper than that. It was a part of me, and I had no fucking clue how to tell Tess that I was a failure to her. That I'd let her down. Let *myself* down. And I only had myself to blame.

When we drove past the turn-off to the barn where we'd stopped and fucked before our picnic, Tess huffed softly, lacing her fingers with mine on the gearshift.

I flinched but didn't tug away. I permitted the contact and even managed to smile while swallowing every agonising thought into my gut.

How did people do this? How did they allow themselves to become so weak and desperate for things they had no right to want? What happened to my cold-hearted bastard self where I needed nothing and no one? Why couldn't I remain such a beast who was satisfied with pain and pleasure from his *esclave*? Why did I have to fucking grow up?

The awful questions kept me company the entire drive. Tess remained silent, petting Courage, who'd fallen asleep and snored on her lap.

When we finally arrived home, the day was done and so was I.

Leaving the chateau staff to unload our belongings and place the Aston Martin back in the garage, I launched myself from the car and waited until Tess passed me the dog. I escorted her inside, took a deep breath, and said, "I need some time alone, *esclave*." Passing her the puppy, I glanced away. "I love you, but please…let me sort myself out on my own. I don't want to take this out on you."

Her chest rose as if preparing for a fight. Her eyes glowed with agony, unable to understand why I wouldn't let her in.

I wanted to.

Fuck, how I wanted to.

But I couldn't do it.

Not yet.

Not looking back or paying any attention to the sudden flurry of dog feet hurtling from the lounge, I strode to the staircase and headed down into the gaming room and my fully stocked cellar of expensive whiskey.

I needed to forget.

I needed to drink…
For just a little while.

Tess

"DO YOU KNOW what's going on, Suzette?"

Suzette tucked dark hair behind her ear, shaking her head. "No idea."

We'd convened in the kitchen—where we always seemed to gravitate—after an uneventful dinner.

Franco spent the evening patrolling the chateau and briefing his security staff on the week ahead. Q hadn't returned from his gaming room meltdown. And Mrs. Sucre had the night off.

I'd hoped Suzette would help me. After all, she'd been key for me understanding Q at the beginning. She had a sixth sense where her employer and friend was concerned. Then again, so did I.

When we'd arrived home, he couldn't wait to be on his own. He couldn't even look at Courage or the other puppies as they came charging from the lounge. Considering he was so attentive and kind to those in need, he didn't relax around the dogs—almost as if their juvenile charm angered him rather than soothed.

They were only dogs. All they wanted was love. He spent hours caring for his birds…so what was the difference?

I spent another few minutes with Suzette, drowning in questions and worry before I retired to my bedroom. Q wasn't there, and I deliberated whether I should encroach on his personal space and demand an explanation.

But he'd promised he would tell me within a week.

The week wasn't up yet.

And I'd vowed to stop being angry and give him space. I didn't want to hurt him when he was already hurting.

So, instead of doing what I wanted, I forced myself to relax in a bath, and when I finally slipped into bed, I stared at the ceiling for hours waiting for Q to join me.

In all the years of our marriage, we'd never slept apart.

I had to trust that tonight would be no different. He would come to bed. He wouldn't shut me out so completely.

I was right.

As the glowing screen of my phone showed two a.m., Q finally entered our tower bedroom. His dark silhouette glowed in stark contrast to the white rug as he stripped dark jeans and black t-shirt and climbed into bed.

I lay there, not wanting to damage an already damaged situation, but I couldn't stomach the silence anymore.

I expected him to be drunk. But no whiskey fumes swirled off him.

I bit my lip.

Damn.

It would've been easy to get a reaction out of him if he'd been drunk. That was how I got him to string me up and fully show me what he was capable of the first time. He unlocked his cage when he consumed alcohol.

As a few minutes ticked past and we lay stiffly side by side, I'd finally had enough.

Sitting up, I turned on the bedside light, grabbed the black bag Q had used in *Castelnaud-des-Fleurs,* and unzipped it.

Q propped himself up on his pillows never taking his eyes off me as I loaded the tattoo gun, reached across and removed his wedding ring. Silently, I requested he hold his hand strong and sure.

Without a word, he obeyed.

He let me turn on the vibrating needle and ink his skin

with the same inscription he'd done for me.

Je suis à toi. I'm yours.

The words made me his possession. But it did the opposite.

I felt as if I tied a rope between us, staking claim once more that he was mine. With every letter I scrawled, I reaffirmed the vow that he belonged to me in sickness and in health, in happiness and in strife. No matter what he was going through or the fear and pain he refused to share, I would be there for him.

When I'd finally finished and placed the now quiet tattoo gun back into the bag, I whispered, "You're mine, Q. I'll be here until you want to talk. And then…when you do, I'll accept whatever it is you're dealing with. We'll get through it together."

Sighing heavily, Q clutched me to his side. "I'm sorry I'm being such a bastard."

"I just wish you'd tell me."

"I will. I promise." Kissing the top of my head, his powerful arm stretched above us and turned out the light.

Darkness cocooned us, reminding me that we'd found each other in this painful black void and made it our home. Q would do anything for me and me for him.

Having his warmth surrounding me finally stole some of my anxiety, and I relaxed into him.

His chest rose and fell, his heartbeat thudding gently against my spine.

I loved this man.

With all my heart and soul.

He was more than just my master and friend—he was my life.

"Je t'aime, Q." I love you.

His arms banded exquisitely tight. *"Je t'aime avec toutes les ombres du monde pour l'éternité."* I love you with all the shadows in the world for eternity.

Sighing, I fell asleep with our bodies entwined.

At least physical distance didn't exist between us anymore. Tomorrow, I'd work on the emotional gap and guide my husband back to me.

I WAS BEING a fucking bastard.

I knew that.

I knew it, but I couldn't change it.

Every time I tried to talk about what hurt me, my throat clammed up and my heart bucked out of control. When Tess had tattooed me last night, she'd given me more than I could've asked for. She gave me time to sort my shit out and the courage in which to do it.

I wouldn't return home without having the balls to get this over with and tell her. She deserved to know, and I deserved to make peace with it so I could move the fuck on with my life.

Placing my wedding ring on the desk (ignoring medical protocol for new tattoo healing just like Tess had), I traced the dainty lettering on my finger left by my incredible wife and wrenched open the locked cupboard beneath the stationary drawer.

I had a private stash for days full of stressful business. I rarely touched it and never thought I'd be stressed where Tess was concerned—not now she was safe and forever mine.

Last night, I had full intentions of getting ridiculously drunk. I'd even taken my time selecting a perfect bottle of liquor. I'd sat in my leather chair and glowered at the pool table where I'd first hurt Tess. But something had stopped me from pouring the first shot.

Yes, I wanted to drink to rid this crushing desire inside me. But I also needed to be an adult. I wasn't a fucking animal—as much as I gave myself that excuse. I was human. I was a man. These new needs had just fucked me up, and it was time to tell them to piss off because I didn't know how else to deal with them.

However, if I drank, that conviction would fade. I might actually get on my knees in front of Tess and tell her everything I'd been keeping a secret. And no fucking way did she need to see me that way. Who knew what she would do when I finally found the spine to tell her.

No, alcohol wasn't the right path last night. I needed to be truly honest with myself and see how deep these new desires went before numbing them.

It'd taken hours. My mind had raced. A headache had formed. But at least an answer had solidified.

Now, I knew.

I knew that it wasn't a superficial dream. Somehow, this craving had become a part of me, and until I knew why I couldn't have what I wanted, I wouldn't give up hope. Sitting downstairs alone, I'd made a deal with my beast.

I promised that if I could collar it for a time, shove its dark needs deep, deep inside me, then perhaps I might be worthy of getting what I wanted.

It was a fucking ridiculous thought. A shrink would have a field day with me. But it was how I felt, what I believed, and nothing would convince me otherwise.

Frederick knocked on my door, letting himself in before I approved—like he always did. The day had been busy, going over a new merger and making sure every last bit of paperwork was finalised for the new investments on our books.

He knew more than I did about what I was going through. Not because I'd told him but because he was the one who'd guessed before I had.

Smug bastard.

Pinching two crystal glasses on the silver tray by my

bookcase, he settled into the Eames chair facing my desk and wiggled the two goblets for me to fill.

I obeyed without speaking.

Pulling the expensive liquor from my cupboard, I sloshed a generous amount into both. Stoppering the bottle, I picked up the cool glass and clinked with his.

With a nod, we threw back the fire.

Hissing between my teeth, I immediately refilled and drank again.

My friend's eyes burned into me.

I wanted him to leave, but he wouldn't. He'd never given me room to mope in my past, and he sure as hell wouldn't now. He believed I'd grown up; lost my diabolical need to hurt. What he didn't know was I was better at negotiating deals with the monster living inside me. Those needs weren't gone. The anger and rage at the filth of the world hadn't faded. If I could trade places with one of the mercenaries I'd hired and kill a few traffickers with my bare hands, I would. I wasn't growing soft in my old age. I was growing more and more lethal.

Tess recognized it.

I recognized it.

It was yet another reason why I'd condemned myself to this future. Because the alternative was too fucking terrifying to contemplate.

"Have you told her yet?" Frederick refilled his glass, keeping pace with me. Thank hell the helicopter was on standby to take me home because we would be over the limit within minutes.

Fuck it.

Last night, I'd restrained myself. I'd had the strength to soul search and compartmentalize what I needed to say to Tess. Tonight was about giving myself some freedom.

If Frederick wanted to drink with me, then fine and fucking dandy. "No."

"Will you tell her?"

"Yes."

"When?"

I shrugged, taking another shot.

"You have to get it out in the open, Q. You've never kept any secrets before." He massaged his neck from working all day. "Besides, she's already guessed. She said she'd seen the paperwork. She's smart."

"I know she's smart. But I've given no indication of wanting this before now. I even told her at the start of our relationship that I didn't want it at all. Why would she put two and two together?"

"Because she's your wife and she loves you. She feels what you do."

I shook my head. "She feels what I *want* her to feel."

Could she have guessed? Would she tell me if she had?

Frederick laughed. "If you believe that, then you're an idiot. Wives know more than us. A lot more." Tapping the paperwork proud and centre on my desk, he added, "This charity proves that you can have what you want just in a different way."

"I don't want it that way."

"Well, it might be the only way unless you man the fuck up and find out once and for all."

I tossed back a double, wincing as the burn incinerated my insides. "I already know what I'm doing wrong."

Frederick paused. "You do?"

I nodded. "I'm hurting her. Whenever we fuck, I go too far. She says she likes it but what if she's lying? What if she'd said no...at the start? Would I have found the strength to stop? Would I be better now?"

"If you start chasing answers to those questions, you'll drive yourself insane." Frederick slowed his drinking while I threw back another and another.

My vision lost its sharpness, but I didn't give a damn. If I had to crawl home, I'd be fine with that.

"I don't need to chase. I have answers."

"Don't torture yourself, Q. That stupid conclusion you

came to last week isn't the reason."

"Fuck, it has to be. What else?"

"Anything more believable, that's what." Frederick suddenly stood up. "You know what? Go home. Talk to your wife. I'm not doing this with you. Only she knows exactly what you guys get up to. She's the one who will tell you you're being a fucking idiot."

I stood up, bracing my fists on the desktop. "Don't call me a fucking idiot."

Frederick chuckled, moving toward the door. "Go home, Q. Talk to her. It's the only thing you can do to get this mess sorted out."

He didn't let me retaliate.

Slipping through the door, he closed it with a soft click.

I itched to throw his empty glass at the wood but refrained. Just.

He was wrong that going home and talking to Tess was the only thing I could do.

I had other alternatives.

Such as sitting here drinking and finding liquid courage to do what was needed.

Forgoing the glass, I tipped the bottle straight to my lips.

Who needed a goblet when it all ended up in my stomach anyway?

Tess

I SMELLED HIM before I heard him.

Even obliterated Q moved like a freaking ghost.

I'd fallen asleep in the library beside the fire. Courage and his family were curled up in the ambient warmth of the flames on the chesterfield rug, snoring lightly, while I reminded myself over and over that Q and I were fine.

For hours, I'd been ensconced with old books and the memories of the past—remembering when I'd returned to Q and taken a blood pledge to always fight him, always stand up to him, and never, ever let him break me.

For some reason, I'd let him pull away these past few days. I'd broken that vow by not fighting. I'd destroyed my side of the bargain because I'd let him win.

But not anymore.

I'd done a lot of thinking about the charity I'd seen on his desk and the reasons for his unhappiness. Seeds of ideas had sprouted into mildly terrifying but scarily exciting conclusions.

I think I know...

Q padded past the library, taking with him the fumes of whiskey. I waited as he patrolled the house, looking for me. Everyone had gone to bed even though it was only eleven p.m.

I was glad for the pretense of an empty home. We had no recovering women living under our roof tonight; the three rehabilitating girls in our current care slept in the house across the lawn with their families.

Which was good.

Because Q and I had a lot to talk about and I wasn't entirely sure how it would end.

When he finally stalked through the premises and didn't find me, he retraced his steps. My skin prickled as his footfalls sounded louder just before his shadow appeared in the doorway. The dog's ears pricked; their black eyes zeroing in on the master of the household.

"There you are, *esclave*."

His voice was heavy and potent, slipping through my blood like the alcohol he'd consumed. I doubted he'd eaten; I hadn't seen him this pissed since the night the police arrived.

My body tingled, remembering what we'd done afterward. How connected we'd been. How in love I'd fallen from one night of unbridled monstrosity.

I wanted that to happen again.

I wanted him angry and rough. I wanted to be completely consumed. And I knew how to make that happen.

Placing the first edition copy of some French classic onto the side table by the wingback, I stood on firm legs. I'd slipped into a pastel pink negligee. My hair was freshly washed with air-dried curls, and my body hid behind the clinging satin, hinting at my curves. My hands curled for war, but my nipples betrayed me, pinpricking like diamonds against the lingerie, very visible and aching for his teeth.

I'd dressed accordingly for the sexual fight we would no doubt commit.

His eyes drifted to my chest, his throat working as he swallowed.

Q had only grown more attractive as he aged.

His sharp widow peak and soft green eyes were severe and pristine. His black suit and aubergine tie crisp and full of dominant authority. From his clipped fingernails to his polished, sharp teeth, Q was a predator through and through.

But I wasn't his prey.

I was his equal. Hunting by his side, massacring our enemies, not afraid to enter a fight with him snarling beside me. But like any good partner, I submitted to him and only him. I sheathed my claws when he came for me. I bit but only gently. I let my mate mount me and fuck me because our power lay in the dynamics of being equals and accepting our place in life.

Our place together.

Q had forgotten his place.

I would help remind him of it.

Ignoring the dogs, I strode to meet him in the middle of the carpet. I tilted my head. His glassy eyes met mine, struggling to focus after drinking copious amounts of whiskey. "Hello, *maître*."

"*Bonsoir.*" Good evening.

His French never failed to lash around me with the softest threads and harshest demands. I shuddered with anticipation and desire. I wanted to give in to him so desperately, but I also wanted to fight.

We *needed* to fight. To air whatever it was that he hurt with.

I wouldn't drag this out. We both knew we'd been stalemate. We hadn't moved past the conversation we were about to have when Frederick had interrupted us.

As if no time had passed, I said, "I saw those papers on your desk. I know the ones you mean."

Q stood ramrod straight. "We're doing this now?"

"Do you have a better idea?"

A cloak of despondency settled over him. "Fine." His fingers moved stealthy, undoing his tailored jacket and slipping it down his arms. Standing with only the slightest wobble, he undid his cufflinks, threw them to the floor, and rolled up his shirt cuffs. His tie was undone and tossed over the arm of the wingback while the first few buttons of his black shirt were undone to reveal a tease of the tattoo on his chest.

I didn't know if he was preparing to talk or attack me.

My breathing turned feathery. Did he have to do that? In just a few motions, he'd made this layered with sex.

"Where do you want to start, Q?"

He chuckled with black undertones, "Oh, I can think of a few places." He stalked me.

I parried back. If I let him touch me, it would be all over. The air crackled with pent-up lust. My voice wobbled. "Why did you get so upset? Why won't you talk to me?"

"First, tell me what you saw."

"I already told you."

"No, you didn't." He shook his head, his eyes flashing. "Along with the animal charities, what else have I donated heavily to?"

My heart chased my lungs around. This was it. I didn't look away. "Orphanages."

His posture stiffened. "And—"

"And supporting unwanted babies with medical issues."

He continued to corral me around the room. "Any idea why I would suddenly have the urge to help in that way after a lifetime of no interest?"

I shrugged, but I couldn't hide the knowledge from blaring on my face.

He kept chasing me, backing me into the same desk that he'd swiped everything off and made me vow to love him no matter what. The polished wood stopped my retreat. He had me trapped. "Q…"

Deleting the space between us, he bared his teeth. "Yes, Tess?"

"I don't know…"

"Yes, you do."

"I need you to say it—"

He chuckled angrily. "No, you don't. According to Frederick, you know more than you've let on."

I do. Or at least, I think I do. But why won't he admit it?

Feigning ignorance, I tried again. "Tell me…"

"Why should I?"

"Because I want the truth."

He snarled. "The truth?"

My spine tensed. "Yes."

Q jerked hands through his hair. "Okay…the truth." Taking a shaking breath, he growled, "I want something I didn't think I'd ever want."

"You want to adopt?"

His glare pinned me into a panting statue. "Try again, *esclave*."

Oh, my God.

I was right.

I'd wondered if this would ever happen. If Q would change his mind about having a family. He said he didn't want one. How could he switch so quickly?

"You want a child?"

He didn't reply, but his eyes glowed a deeper, truer green full of confession and guilt.

Why did he feel guilty? There was nothing to be guilty about. People changed their minds all the time.

My hastily formed conclusions from earlier turned from seedlings into thick roots threading through my heart.

A family…

"Is that true?"

His eyes dove into mine. "As much as I wish it wasn't, yes, it's true."

"You're helping with charities because your mind has turned to babies."

A black cloud descended over him. "And what does that tell you, Tess?"

"You want a baby?"

His face hardened. "With?"

"With me?" My fingers fluttered over my chest. I wobbled at the thought of getting everything I'd ever dreamed of. I'd accepted his condition about not having children because I loved him enough to be complete without it. But hearing him admit to a change of heart…

I couldn't explain the fizzing giddy sensation making its way through my blood.

I wanted to touch him, hug him...finally tell him my opinions about such a revelation. *Imagine sharing our wonderful life with a child of our own...wow.* Even though I'd known Q's stance on starting a family, it didn't mean I hadn't tested his conviction over a year ago.

Dinner one night, I'd brought it up—very suave with no pressure—and Q hadn't been interested in the slightest. I'd remained on my contraception injections and didn't mention it again.

He'd been through a lot with his family, and I hadn't had the best experience, either. If he didn't want children, then I wouldn't pressure him. I hadn't brought it up again, which made this all the more precious because he'd come to this realisation on his own with no prompting or hinting from me.

He hadn't replied.

I repeated my breathless question. "You're saying you want a baby with me?"

Trembling, Q placed his hands on either side of me, hemming me against the desk. His eyes shot black, dropping to my lips as the heart-stopping words spilled from his lips. "More than fucking anything."

"But...I don't understand."

"What's there to understand? I've had a change of heart. I never wanted kids, and now...now, I want it more than fucking anything because I love you. I want to multiply you. I want you pregnant with my, *our* child."

Tears glossed my eyes. "But when we talked about it before you said—"

"I didn't want this then."

"So...what's changed?"

His gaze devoured me. "Me, you. Us. Everything. Can't I change my mind about such things?"

I wanted to look away but couldn't. My skin tingled with intensity. "But I'm on birth control. The injection doesn't fade for another few months."

Q reared back, yet another secret inscribed on his face.

"Tess—"

For a moment, anger heated me. What had he done? But then fear filled me instead. Pushing off from the desk, I followed him. "What is it? What do you know that I don't?"

Was he infertile? Did he have a vasectomy before we met? *What?*

Dropping his gaze, he muttered, "You've been off contraception for two months."

I stopped breathing. *"What?"*

"The last appointment you had..." He stomped away, his voice full of emotion. "I know I shouldn't have done it. But I wanted to see. I *needed* to see. If I got you pregnant, I would've been free to love you the way I have. I would've been fucking ecstatic."

I wrapped my arms around myself suddenly icy cold. "You had the doctor give me a placebo? Q...why would you do such a thing? What if I'd changed my mind and no longer wanted children? What if I was on contraception because I agreed with you about keeping our family just the two of us?"

Q froze. "You have every fucking right to be angry at me."

"Angry? I'm livid!" My hands balled. "You did that behind my back! For months, you've been feeling this way and only now you tell me? What would you have done if I *had* fallen pregnant, huh? Would you have told me that you deliberately knocked me up or lie about it being an accident? Would you have made me feel terrible for trapping you into something you didn't want believing the injection failed?"

I couldn't look at him.

Tearing past, I charged for the door. I needed some space, to get my head on so I didn't say something I regretted.

But he didn't let me.

His hand lashed out, fingers locking around my wrist. "You're not going anywhere, *esclave*. You're the one who wanted to talk."

"Talk, yes. But not discover you've been lying to me for weeks!"

"I'm sorry for—"

"For not sharing this with me? Don't you think this should've been discussed when you first started feeling this way? What on earth were you thinking, Q? How *dare* you tamper with my medical appointment!"

Served me right for using the doctor Q vetted and approved. Client confidentiality, my ass. Ugh, I felt so betrayed.

Q didn't let me go, waiting for my temper to blow itself out. However, my mind filled with other complications. Worse complications. I stiffened as realisation kicked into me.

Q understood where my thoughts had gone. His shoulders slouched. "Now, do you get it?"

No, I didn't get it. But I had a lot more questions trying to understand.

I hugged myself. "If what you said is true, and I've been off contraception for two months…why haven't I become pregnant?"

His eyes glowed with agony, moving away from me.

It was my turn to chase him. "We've had a lot of sex since then, Q, with no protection. If it were going to happen, it would've happened by now."

At least…I think?

How long did it take the chemical hormones to leave my system? Was my cycle capable of conception or screwed after using contraception for so long? And if it wasn't, what did that mean? Was it just a time thing or was it something a lot, lot worse.

My heart squeezed as Q shook his head, his face tight and hard. I'd gone straight to the crux of his pain. The issue he'd been dealing with alone without talking to me.

He stormed away, pinching the bridge of his nose. "That's what's been fucking with my head."

"What do you mean?"

"I mean…what if our lifestyle—the way we have sex— means you can't get pregnant? What if when I hurt you, your body refuses my cum because it's nature's way of preventing life from entering a world that's so violent."

"What? That's insane." I couldn't stop rolling my eyes. "That's the most stupidest—"

Slamming to a stop, he grabbed me. "It's not stupid. It's fucking karma." His fingers dug into my arms far tighter than required. "I've killed so many. I've hurt others. Been a fucking animal." He sneered at his hold. "See, I can't even hold you without wanting to hurt you. What sort of home is that for a kid to be born into? It's my fault you can't get pregnant. I'm the one who whips you and does god-awful shit to you. This is my punishment for loving you so goddamn much but unable to give you everything you want because I take so much from you. I'm being punished because of the fucked-up part of me I can't control."

I buckled beneath his pain even as a disbelieving laugh fell from my lips. "Oh, my God. You've lost it. You're afraid of what you'll do to your children because of what we do together? I'll tell you what you'd do. You'd dote upon them, Q. You'd be the best, protective father who only had their well-being in mind. You're one of the most selflessly kind people I know—"

"You don't know the urges I fight every day, Tess."

"No, and you don't know mine. If you did, there is no way you could believe such filth."

We breathed hard, glowering at each other. I wanted to hit him; to try and strike some sense into that thick skull. Instead, I did my best to keep my temper in check.

Inhaling deeply, I whispered, "You have to stop torturing yourself. All of that is ludicrous. You're insane to believe that."

"Don't deny that I'm not a good person, Tess. The things I've done—"

I bared my teeth. "Whatever badness lives inside you, Q, is far outweighed by the good. And if you're blaming yourself based on our choice to add pain to our pleasure, stop that right now. I ask for that. I *live* for that. I love you *because* of that."

He shook his head. "That wasn't what I meant, and you

know it."

I hated to see him so tortured. "If you're saying I want a child… then yes, I do. I love the thought of a son who looks like you. But I also don't cry myself to sleep at night thinking I'll never be complete without one. I *am* complete. *You* make me complete." My hand landed on his chest, his wild heartbeats drumming in my fingertips. "Don't destroy yourself with those thoughts. What we have together—the violent love we share— it isn't just you who indulges. I'm a full participant. Besides, that isn't the reason why we aren't getting pregnant—"

"Oh? Why else would it fucking be? Am I sterile then? Am I the one to blame for that, too?"

"No!" My heart matched his as I cupped his cheek. "You're never to blame. Never, do you hear me? You said it yourself, it's only been two months. That's nothing in the scheme of things. We'll get tested…find out why and go from there."

He lied to me for two months. He'd been living with these nonsensical thoughts, falling deeper and deeper into their falsehoods.

I wish he'd talked to me sooner. Perhaps then he wouldn't be such a foolish man believing in preposterous notions that he was the one to blame because of his desires.

How anyone could think that was beyond me. But this was Q. He'd sent me back to Brax because of the same reason. The reason hidden beneath his self-hatred, doubts, and guilt.

That he'll never be pure enough to deserve me, our love…a family.

"Tests?" He reared back. "No."

The thought of doctors prodding and invasive examinations wasn't something I was keen to do, but if he wanted a family as much as he said he did, then that was what had to happen.

Something switched in him, shedding the fight and becoming sharp with conviction. His face contorted, his drunken haze granting fake lucidity. "I have a better idea."

"Oh?"

"All our years together, we've given into the inner-most urges. When we fuck, it's intense and almost life threatening with how deep we go. Your body is too focused on staying alive to let the natural progression of whatever it is that makes you pregnant." He grabbed me by the back of the nape. "I want to try something different. I want to make love to you, Tess."

What is he talking about?

"You do. Every time we're together." *Doesn't he know that love drenches his every touch?* "You *do* make love to me, Q."

He chuckled. "No, I make war with you. I fuck you. I adore you. I ruin you. For too long I've been weak, thinking I couldn't change who I was. I need to pay a toll or find redemption...*something* to make me a better person."

Ugh, I can't get through to him like this.

I was stubborn. But Q was a concrete wall. If he believed these daft ideas, it would take days, possibly weeks to refute them and change his mind. However, it was possible. I'd done it before when I returned to him. I would do it again.

My heart galloped around my ribcage. "I don't know what you're talking about. None of that makes sense. You're being absurd."

"Absurd?" His face blackened. "You think I'm absurd when I share my innermost fears? That it's okay to roll your eyes and laugh at me? Fuck, Tess. I can't rationalize the way I feel. I know how moronic it sounds. But I need to do this. I have to try. Otherwise, I'll hate myself more than I already do."

I sucked in a breath. "You don't mean that."

"Je déteste ne pas être un homme meilleur. Oui." I hate that I'm not a better man. Yes.

"Take that back, Q."

He sighed heavily, reaching out to touch me. "Tess, please, don't judge. You've let me do all manner of shit to you. The one time I ask to worship you and you fight me." His head bowed. "Please don't fucking fight me."

I didn't know how to take this. *What is he saying?* How had he twisted himself into so many unfathomable knots?

Courage whined from his place on the rug, interrupting our heavy argument. Taking a deep breath, I truly studied Q. His face was drawn with dark angles. His eyes haunted and lost. If he fully believed in such silly things, who was I to belittle them? The only way to prove he was wrong. To remind him he was a wonderful, selfless man was to give in.

For just a little while.

Moving closer to him, I murmured. "If you need to do whatever it is you're saying, I won't say no. However, I don't believe it has anything to do with—"

"This is what has to happen, *esclave*. Do I need to tie you down to make it come true?"

My lips curled. "That sounds more like the man I married."

He refused to smile in return, his eyes crackling with lust. "I'm going to worship you. I'm not going to hurt you or drag you into pain. But not tonight."

My insides turned to liquid at the thought of connection and sex. I wanted him. Especially now he'd added an entirely new element to our marriage. "Why not tonight?" I waved at the empty house, encompassing the canine witnesses by the fire. "We have the space to ourselves." *Minus a few doggy voyeurs.*

Slipping into the monstrous master I knew, he growled, "Because right now, I have a much better idea. If I'm going to do this. If I'm going to shackle the beast inside and treat you the way you've always meant to be treated, then I need one more night. I need to fuck you, Tess. I need it raw with no limits. Let me take that from you and I'll give you everything else I can in return."

I shivered. "You don't have to convince me. I want what you do. We don't have to stop—"

His hand smashed over my lips. "Yes, we do. I'm being punished for the way I treat you. It's only right. What sort of fucking parent would I be if our baby was born to a mother with bruises? What sort of father would I be if I dreamed of making you bleed? I have to get rid of that part of me. It's not right. It's not human. And I need to be human to deserve you. To deserve a *child* with you."

His voice plaited with rage and despair.

There was no talking him out of such crazy rationale. There was no right and wrong. No law or rules that said we couldn't indulge in what we wanted and still have a family. Q was the most protective man; he would be the best father imaginable. What we did together behind closed doors was no one else's business, including any children we might have.

To imagine him taking that away from me—forbidding any more violent lust was blasphemous.

If he weren't already drunk, I would've made him so. If he went through with this idiotic idea, I wanted him to lose all control tonight. I wanted to be completely and utterly at his mercy with no thoughts between us.

Nothing but touch and trembles.

Pressing on my breastbone, Q walked me backward to the desk. Never removing his fingers, he shoved me hard, gritting his teeth as I splayed over the desk. Behind me sat an untouched plate of strawberry jam and fresh scones that a maid had brought in for dessert.

I hadn't touched it.

Q noticed the edible confectionary instantly. "Ever heard the expression 'you shouldn't play with your food?'" His hand shot over my head, his fingers digging into the red sugar preserve. Never breaking eye contact, he brought the sweetness to my cheek.

Smearing it on my overheated skin, he smiled. "We're about to break that rule."

Uncertainty and excitement bubbled in my blood. I'd won this fight, and Q had finally talked to me. But I hadn't won at all because if he went through with this, then he would take away a part of him that I was madly in love with.

Already, I mourned our violent affair, and he hadn't even muzzled himself yet.

Q hovered above me, his body wound tight and bristling with lust. His pale eyes spoke of nothing but the urge to dominate and fuck.

With infinitesimal slowness, he inserted the sticky strawberry jam on his finger into my mouth. His wedding ring glinted in the low light, hinting at the inked tattoo beneath the gold.

I moaned as his finger hooked over my tongue, yanking my mouth open before crashing his lips over mine and kissing me deep and wet and true.

Breaking our connection, his tongue licked my cheek, taking the rest of the jam before kissing me again with sugary seduction.

I shuddered against him, life fading around us, as he became my sun and gravity.

My throat ached as his fingers dropped to strangle me. His large hand bordered delicate and crushing as the tiny urge to scratch and fight waged with submitting and begging for more.

Q fought himself on a minutely basis. For him to finally admit he wanted a family proved he was capable of so much more than he believed.

A child would weaken and empower him. A son would keep him fighting and possessive for years. And a daughter…a daughter might just ruin him with his desire to keep her safe.

But he was willing to drive himself mad because the urge inside overpowered his reason. It made me love him all the more. Our relationship had started on a quicksand foundation, slowly growing firmer as we grew to trust each other and accept what we needed. Now that foundation was stone and granite. He could have me like this and be a good father.

I just had to show him that. Just like I'd taught him so many things in our time together.

"Come." Q let my throat go, breaking the kiss and pulling me from the desk.

I swallowed around the slight bruising of my larynx, blinking back swirling need. "Where are we—"

"No questions." His face darkened as he escorted me from the library.

With our hands interlocked, he guided me down the corridor to the indoor swimming pool.

We used this place often. I loved to exercise in the mornings and indulge in a few laps before breakfast. Q preferred to work out at night, removing the stress of the day and any other problems in his mind before obliterating the rest of his concerns by making love to me.

He doesn't believe what we do is making love.

Silly, silly man.

It was. Through and through.

I touched my bruised lips, tasting strawberry jam as Q locked the door, leaving us in echoey silence with the tang of salt in the air. The pool wasn't chlorinated but kept clean and filtered using liquid as salty as the sea.

His eyes flashed with shame before being swallowed by blazing darkness. "Tonight, there are no rules, *esclave. As-tu un problème avec ça?*" Do you have a problem with that?

My body loosened, melted, giving into his wishes before he'd even begun. Q's ferocity was gasoline to the already curling fire turning my blood into dust. "No."

"Good."

Removing the distance between us, Q placed both hands on my cheeks. His fingers would've been loving and tender, but they bit with silent need. "I'm going to fuck you, wife."

I sucked in a hopeless breath as Q bowed his head and kissed me.

His tongue lashed out with demand, forcing me to follow his lead. I tensed for pain, for a bite or claw, but he kept himself sweet. The kiss granted a false sense of security and romance as his hands left my face, dancing over my breasts.

Arching my back, I pressed my nipples into his touch, moaning for more.

His lips tightened in a feral smile beneath mine as he ignored my request and moved his fingers to my shoulders.

He hovered there.

Kissing me.

Loving me.

I didn't move.

Knowing this wasn't the end but merely the beginning, I held my ground as Q looped his touch beneath the spaghetti straps of my negligee. With a harsh breath, he tore at the material.

I cried out in pain as the satin cut into my shoulder blades, fighting his desire to destroy it.

The nightgown put up a fight, but it was useless.

Q wanted me naked.

He wanted to butcher my outer shell and strip me nude because he couldn't hurt my flesh in the same way. This was his only outlet, and I had no problem replacing yet another negligee with new.

My stomach flipped as his lips landed on my brand, his hand fisting my hair to tilt my head the way he needed. He licked me, keeping his teeth sheathed as my nightgown slipped to the damp floor.

The air inside the pool dripped with humidity. The carving of jungle and parrots decorating the walls were the only witnesses as I stood naked and wanting.

Our breaths were lost in the liquid music of a waterfall spilling into the pool, leaving the water rippling and broken.

Taking my hand, Q paced toward the control panel where light switches and temperature gauges rested. Selecting only one form of illumination, I smiled as the LED lights in the pool sprang bright. Hidden at the bottom they filtered through the water, bouncing of crimson mosaic and turning the salty depths a blood, blood red.

Q smiled as he guided me toward the shallows. "Get in."

Not giving me a choice, he pushed.

I stepped off the edge and held my breath as the warm water lapped over my head. Pushing off from the bottom, I broke the surface and wiped away droplets to watch Q undress.

Not that Q undressed.

He tore like a beast shedding its winter coat.

He was as violent with his own clothes as he was with mine. Ripping his shirt, not caring about buttons, and tearing at his fly to kick away expensive shoes and tailored suits. The minute he was naked, he stood over me proud and glorious.

Taking his cock in his hand, he stroked the steel-hard length. "Take a good look, Tess. Because soon this will be so far inside you, you'll be screaming for mercy."

Water cascaded off my arm as I reached for him. "Can I touch you?"

"Tu peux me sucer si tu le souhaites." You can suck if you wish.

I licked my lips. "I do wish." Shivering, I couldn't look away from him. I stared at both my husband and the monster I would never be able to tame. To think Q would try to shackle this part of himself and win? It was inconceivable. He was wild at heart. It would break him to be normal.

"You have to come closer, *maître*." My eyes dropped to his lips. They were wet from his tongue, making my mouth water at the thought of kissing him again.

Never looking away, Q bent his knees until he crashed on the edge of the pool. His fingers grew white as he fisted his cock. "I'll only ever accept instruction from you, my sweet wife." His free hand dropped to my nipple, tugging it hard. "You have me on my knees. What do you intend to do with me?"

My breathing turned shallow as I pressed my body against the side of the pool. My mouth was so close to his erection—a willing vessel ready to taste.

But I paused.

Fluttering my eyelashes, I whispered, "My intention, dear master, is to suck your cock until you snap. I want to taste the whiskey you've been drinking, I want to bite you so you rage, and then, when you've had enough of my mouth, I want you to fuck me like you were born to do."

His jaw clenched; his five o' clock shadow darker in this

gloomy water world. Letting go of his cock, he grabbed my head, bringing me toward him. "When you talk like that, how am I supposed to say no?" His teeth flashed as his touch turned brutal, inserting his hot erection past my lips. "Suck me like a good little *esclave*."

My tongue swiped around his crown. We groaned in unison.

Once upon a time, I'd taken it upon myself to break Q. Believing, that until he gave in to me and trusted my love for him, he'd never be free. This reminded me so much of that. He wanted something more from me. Something I was achingly ready to give. But he was afraid.

And Q afraid was not a good thing. He would be volatile, mercurial, and impossible to predict.

Slackening my jaw, I inserted his length past my gag reflex.

Q half-grunted, half-growled as I cupped his balls and squeezed. His body swayed forward, teetering on the edge of the pool while I stood waist deep in warm water and sucked him.

I knew how he liked it. I knew what turned him on.

I hummed low in my throat.

The vibration of my voice rippled over his erection, activating the muscles in his lower belly. Q breathed hard, sending his sparrow tattoo fluttering like crazy.

He groaned as he fisted himself, working deeper into my mouth. "Fuck, I want to climb inside you."

I pulled away for a second. "Get into the pool and do it. Please, God, do it."

"So fucking demanding tonight." He throttled his length. "I don't remember agreeing to obey you."

"You obey me because I am your wife."

His face arranged into a roguish smile. "And my wife needs to remember her place."

Pointing at his glistening cock, a small droplet of pre-cum hovered on the tip. "You haven't finished with your first task." His balls sat high and tight, straining with the urge to come.

Reaching for my hair again, he jerked my face onto his erection. "Use your pretty mouth for more important things, *esclave*." With powerful hands, he gripped my nape, locking me into the perfect position to be used.

I shivered.

Our eyes burned holes in each other, but we didn't say a word.

I inched higher, opening my mouth and latching my fingers around him.

His head fell back, as I slipped him onto my tongue. "Goddammit, Tess."

I opened wide and sucked Q deep, deep, *deep*. He threaded his fingers tighter into my hair, holding me prisoner as my tongue lapped and licked.

He rocked into me, pressing down on my head. "Take it. Fuck."

My pussy clenched. I saw stars with how much I wanted him inside me. My teeth teased his velvety skin, hinting at my need to consume him.

His cock rippled as I sucked harder.

He shuddered as I sank back down on him, waiting for him to snap, sliding my hand once again between his legs and caressing his balls.

He twitched as his muscular thighs quivered.

I flexed my fingers, ignoring everything but getting Q to lose control.

"Fuck, Tess." Q trembled. "I'm so damn close."

My mouth leaked saliva, unable to do anything but accept Q's thrusts. Curses rained in the muggy humidity as his body fought my possession and battled to release.

His body jerked as I sucked particularly hard, determined to drive him to the brink. However, his fingers yanked my head up with danger in his gaze.

I held eye contact as his face contorted with need. "Fuck, you're too good, too pure, too beautiful." His teeth shone in the darkness. "Fucking your mouth, your body…every part of you gets me so fucking hard."

His dirty eloquence puddled into the pool, raising goosebumps on my arms as he jerked me onto his cock. I became more than his wife and pleasure slave. I became his fantasy as he used me.

Throwing his head back, the first taste of salty musk coated my tongue. Instantly, Q shoved me away. I fell backward, disappearing under the water for a moment.

When I stood, he'd launched himself into the pool and shoved me against the mosaic wall. His teeth clamped onto my collarbone as he thrust his cock against my slippery lower belly. "What were you trying to do, *esclave*? Make me come in your mouth rather than your cunt? Do you not want me to get you pregnant?"

I never thought I'd hear Q say such things.

It made me freaking ecstatic.

I panted as he turned me around, squashing me between his rock-stone body and the wall. Water sloshed everywhere as my hands scrambled at the side, concrete biting into my cheek. "No, I do."

Tugging away my soaking wet curls, he bit the back of my neck like a wolf. "Tell me how much you want it."

"I want it. I want you inside me."

"And?"

"I want you to get me pregnant."

"Why?" Grabbing my jaw, he forced me to kiss him. Angling my neck so he could plunder my mouth from behind. The kiss lasted long enough to make me lightheaded and wobbly. If he weren't holding me so tight, I would've floated away like a shipwreck. "Because I want your child."

He jolted, deepening the kiss until I almost gagged. My heart sunburst in my chest as our bodies slicked against each other with war but our mouths dedicated themselves to utmost pleasure.

Breaking away, Q grunted, "You have no idea what that does to me." Running his cock up and down the crack of my ass, he gripped my hip with his free hand. "Feel how hard I am for you, Tess? Feel how much I need to fuck you?"

I nodded, pressing my forehead on the edge of the pool. "Yes."

Words to demand that he do exactly that hovered on my tongue. But I'd learned the hard way. I couldn't control Q's pace. I merely had to give in, let go, and grant total power to him.

I never found that a hardship. More like a sensual gift only he could bestow. I fought so hard to be where I was. I'd done things I wasn't proud of and continued to fight life on everyday concerns. But when I was with Q…none of that mattered. He took every worry and consumed me.

He was more than a master. He was a magician.

Q removed his touch and swam off down the pool. His precise strokes sliced through the water like a blade, his sleek naked form so damn erotic in the welcoming darkness.

I didn't breathe as he reached the other end and effortlessly hauled himself out. Dripping wet and still hard, he stalked toward the changing room where he disappeared for a few seconds before coming out with two things hidden in his hands.

With a sinful smile, he dove back into the water and powered toward me.

I blinked as he swam around me, breaking the surface only once his arm locked around my waist and his hot mouth licked my spine.

Before I could ask what he'd gone to claim, he wrenched my arms behind my back and secured them tightly.

My senses zeroed in on where he touched me, trying to guess what he'd used as a restraint. *I have no idea.* My voice rippled around the pool room. "What are you using?"

Spinning me to face him, his eyes captured mine. "The elastic band you aqua train with."

I squirmed against the tight binding. The thick rubber that acted as a resistance while performing water yoga kept me pinioned. There was no way I could get free.

My heart leapt into my throat. I didn't mind being bound—I loved it. But never in a pool where drowning was entirely too easy, especially in this large space where the bottom shelved steeply into a deep, threatening tide.

"Don't struggle. You know I'll keep you safe." Q's murmur danced down my back.

My panic receded as trust billowed fast and true.

Q was born into darkness, but he'd never baptized me in his blackest desires. And because of that, I could implicitly say he spoke the truth. No matter what he did to me, he would never truly harm me.

Q paused, his tattooed chest soaking. His feathered sparrows fluffing off droplets almost alive on his skin. "I told you once never to fall for me. That I didn't want the curse of breaking your heart while I broke so many other pieces of you." His hands landed on my breasts, cupping them reverently. "Yet you fought me, just like you said you would. You fell for me, just like you promised you would. And now, you're willing to give me what I need even after I tricked you and lied."

I swayed as I fell even deeper for this complex husband of mine. Q was all my fantasies in one glorious lifetime. The fact he finally wanted to share me with his child spoke volumes about his capacity to love.

"I'm so glad you ignored me, *esclave*." His fingertips branded my nipples with pain. "So fucking happy you married me." Pushing me backward, he smiled harshly as my spine met the pool wall. His chest strained as he sucked in a heavy breath. "You're so fucking beautiful."

My heart hammered in my ears as he kissed me.

His tongue laced with mine, and I sank into the sweet embrace, knowing it would be the last I received tonight. The air crackled with an impending storm. Q's control frayed every second, his eyes drenching in determination and the salacious need to hurt.

Breaking the kiss, he opened his hand, revealing the other item he'd retrieved.

A tiny pair of silver scissors from the toiletries in the changing room. I stiffened but didn't flinch. This was Q's signature. It wouldn't be sex with him if he didn't draw a little of my blood.

Gently, he placed the sharp twin blades against my breast just above my nipple. "If I get you pregnant, these won't belong just to me anymore." He pressed down, never breaking eye contact. My skin gave way, permitting a small puncture and blood to well. "Do you think that's fair, *esclave*?"

I moaned as he ducked his head and sucked the bright red bead. His tongue swirled around my nipple, his teeth biting with ruthless sharpness.

Blood raced faster in my veins, either rushing toward him or running away. I could never tell when he put me in this mindset.

"No, they'll always be yours."

"Always?"

"Always, *maître*."

Towering over me, water decorated his face as his hand disappeared beneath the surface to my lower belly. I stopped breathing as the scissors teased my delicate flesh.

"I cut you once here. Do you remember?"

I nodded. "Yes. You licked me clean and then permitted me to do the same to you."

His eyes blackened. "And you liked it? Tasting me? Claiming me?"

My moan was answer enough as he cut me shallow and quick.

We both looked below the surface, fascinated by the slow curl of pink staining from me, vanishing almost instantly into the stinging salt.

"You bleed for me so willingly, Tess." His lips latched around my ear. "Will you scream for me, too?"

My eyes shot wide as his body crushed me against the wall.

My arms bellowed as my bound hands crashed against the tiles. Q ripped my legs from the pool bottom holding my weight as he wrapped my thighs around his hips.

His hand fumbled between us as he angled his cock and shoved deep inside me.

He hadn't touched me there yet. It made the invasion all that more intense.

His face contorted with furious etches. "I'm tired of lying. I'm tired of fighting how much I want this. I'm tired of pretending I don't need this from you." His mouth claimed mine, kissing me hungrily as our bodies connected with no barriers. "I'm giving up. I'm going to do whatever it takes. I'm going to fuck you, love you, win you. And when you're so fucking tired of me taking you, I'm going to do it all over again. You're going to give me what I want. Aren't you, wife?"

His thick cock stole all coherency.

I nodded.

That was all I was capable of. My mouth stretched wide, focusing on the slip and slide of him. The pinch and pain as he fucked me hard. And the glorious pleasure he invoked.

I'd never felt more alive than when we came together. Sex wasn't just for us. It was about making something *from* us. Combining our souls to create another.

It added a terrifying dimension to our sexual fight.

"Yes," I whispered.

Q gritted his teeth, visibly shuddering. He kissed me again. Hard. Fast. Lethal. His hands landed on the edge of the pool, blocking me in the cage of his body while his hips thrust into mine.

I couldn't move. My hands remained locked together, and my neck protested as his kiss turned vicious. He took and gave and took some more. Every twist of his tongue demanded I do what I promised and find a way to become pregnant for him.

Spearing my tongue with his, we battled until we were heaving and insane. Nothing existed but our kiss and being inside each other. The stinging cuts on my breast and stomach only anchored me more to him, and my pussy fired with the need to release, building and building with a demand I couldn't ignore.

"Q…please…I'm going to—"

Instantly, he stopped. Pulling out of me, he ended both the kiss and our connection.

No!

My eyes shot wide with frustration. "Why—why did you stop?"

"Because I don't want you coming without doing something."

Uh-oh.

"Doing what?"

His grin was pure animal. "This."

Taking a deep breath, he vanished beneath the water.

I gasped as his hands pinned my hips against the side of the pool. I teetered with imbalance, unable to hold onto anything with my wrists tied.

What the hell is he doing?

His reply came a second later in the form of teeth.

The wet room ricocheted with my breathless scream as Q's tongue replaced the silk of seawater with sensual saliva. I turned legless and inhuman as he shot his tongue inside me, fucking me just as roughly as he did before.

His fingers replaced his tongue, three stretching me, heralding my begging orgasm.

I gave into him. I didn't have a choice.

My head lolled as his fingers drove in and out and his mouth suckled on my clit. I didn't know how long he could hold his breath, but my shoulders ached and the mental tally it took to stand up while all I wanted to do was melt battled with the spooling sensation in my womb.

And then pain.

My release switched from building to detonating as Q's teeth sank hard and unforgiving into my clit.

He bit me!

My vision blurred on the dark shadow of him beneath the water between my legs. My thighs fought to come together as the most shattering orgasm ripped through me.

His fingers worked me in time, and the softest trickle of blood once again plaited with the pool.

The first, second, third band of my orgasm wrenched me dry, but Q didn't stop tormenting me. He licked and bit until he wrung every shudder from me.

Only then did he push off the bottom and join me on the surface.

He smiled, water rushing off his dark hair and over his sinfully handsome features. "Did you enjoy your release, *esclave*?" His teeth flashed with the barest hint of my blood.

My cheeks blushed and my nipples tingled, calling for the same rough treatment. For Q to say I permitted him to hurt me only because *he* wanted it was absolute filth. I got off on him biting me. I got off on being hurt. It killed me to think of him taking that away from me.

Please, don't ever change.

"Don't ever stop, Q."

He swallowed hard, staring unrepentant. "Don't talk about that now."

My thoughts raced. Even though Q had evolved in our years together, he still needed the primal depth of pain and scars. What would it do to him if he prevented that desire?

My legs trembled with the awful thought of growing apart. He said I was enough. But now he wanted more. What if that more was what broke us?

Q didn't give my worry time to consume me. Grabbing my nape, he yanked me forward to kiss. The faint taste of copper tainted our embrace as he once again hoisted my legs around his waist and slid deep inside me. My back connected with the wall as oxygen fled my lungs.

He never broke the kiss, but I kept my eyes wide open. Focusing on his sculptured cheekbones and how achingly desperate his gaze appeared. We never looked away as his lips worked mine, soft but demanding. His hips rocked with perfect discipline. I moaned as he pressed his muscular body harder against me. The pool heated as our naked skin flushed hotter and hotter.

He withdrew, his cock only an inch inside me.

We stayed like that for a second. Just living in a perfect heartbeat.

Then violence reentered our lovemaking, and my spine arched as he plunged inside me.

Deep.

Hard.

Excruciatingly blissful.

The way he took me held no remnants of our argument or uncertainty. There was no fear or questions. Only the knowledge we belonged to each other forever.

Every time he thrust, I pushed back to meet him. Water splashed all around us, licking up the sides of the pool and echoing in the space. My lungs strained as Q grunted and rutted, taking me deep and thorough.

My hands ached to touch him. To dig my fingernails into his ass and scratch long bloody trails down his spine. I wanted to make him bleed. I wanted to love and adore him, autograph and implore him.

My pussy swelled for another release, heating and begging as a swirling orgasm started in my heart, working its way through my nerve endings.

"Take me, Tess. Every last inch of me." Q bit my ear, losing finesse as he chased what we both needed. His hands roamed every inch—squeezing my thighs, my hips, my breasts. When he rolled my nipples, the percolation inside turned into a nucleus inside my core, just waiting for the final spark to unleash.

My heart rate ratcheted as I fought for pleasure.

"Christ, you look stunning like this. Wet and panting. Bare and begging."

My legs wrapped tighter around his waist as he increased

his speed. His hand dove between us, rubbing my tender, bitten clit. "I want to come, *esclave*. I want to fucking come so bad inside you."

I flinched as intensity became my enemy.

Discomfort flared in my shoulders as my back arched for more.

Words were forgotten as Q lost himself in me. I willingly threw away any decorum or rules and chased him into the darkness.

He pinched my pussy, sending me up the final rungs of my release.

"Fuck. Fuck, yes." His lips pulled back as he jerked into me with short, savage thrusts. His body went taut as he stopped fighting and let go.

The splash of his pleasure inside was the last element I needed to come a second time.

I combusted.

The orgasm thundered into being, webbing on the knife edge of pain, then crescendoing in a shower of sparks. My entire body contracted as I writhed on Q, milking him of everything he had left.

We didn't speak as we stood there, twitching as the final ripples of our bliss faded. The pool slowly calmed from the tidal splashes we'd created and the little pieces of my soul collided with his, acknowledging that this was the start of something bigger than us.

Q chuckled, still rock hard inside. "If you keep clenching around me, Tess, I might have to fuck you again."

My smile was lazy and sated. "I wouldn't say no."

Shadows entered his gaze as he kissed me softly. "The next time, I won't hurt you. I won't bind you, cut you—do anything to make you fear me."

Before I could tell him I had no intention of letting him do such a thing, he pulled out and spun me around. With the scissors he'd nicked me with, he sliced my yoga band and freed me.

As I rubbed circulation back into my wrists, he kissed my throat. His face etched with confliction and heavy self-loathing. "I love you, Tess. And because of that, I won't touch you that way again."

Instead of being content and in love after a soul-deep connection, I felt stranded and alone.

Couldn't he see I didn't want him to pull away?

Couldn't he see he hurt me more saying such things than he ever could with his scissors?

Not giving me a chance to argue, Q swam to the side and climbed out.

He didn't look back.

LAST NIGHT.

Fuck, I shouldn't have gotten that drunk. I shouldn't have come home with frustration in my heart. I had no control over the bastard inside when I did.

I rolled over in bed, drinking in Tess's sleepy form. Her skin glowed with a mixture of marks and bruises, but as she roused beneath my gaze, her smile was sleepy and sexy as she stretched like a well-petted cat. The two small cuts on her breast and belly mocked me.

I daren't look between her legs where I'd bitten her hard enough to break her delicate skin.

"Morning."

I grunted in response, nursing a headache and the awful taste of regret. Swinging my legs out of bed, I massaged my temples. "If I hurt you in the pool, I'm sorry."

Sheets rustled as she crawled toward me. Her warm nakedness draped over my back as she looped her arms around my chest. Her lips landed on my cheek. "Q…I thought we'd discussed this way before we got married. You can't hurt me. I have a safe word if it ever gets too much and I trust you to stop if I ever say it." Her arms banded tighter. "Nothing you did last night was too much. I loved every second of it."

I did my best to shrug her off, standing naked over her. "And what of the other thing we discussed." I pinched the bridge of my nose, doing my best to get my wayward emotions under control. "What of that?"

Tess stood on her knees, proudly displaying the body that I'd coveted, claimed, and ultimately couldn't get pregnant.

Two months.

That was my dirty fucking secret. For two months, I'd slept with my wife, all the while knowing she wasn't on contraception.

Every time I came inside her, I thought she'd come to me with the shy but happy news.

I begged for that day.

I dreamed of her telling me she carried my baby.

But her period kept fucking coming, renouncing me as a man, proving I didn't have what it took to knock her up.

She sighed. "I want a child, too. And I'm willing to do what it takes to make that happen."

A huge gust of relief filled me. Relief that was so fucking opposite to my normal opinion of families and offspring. But with her…everything about me had changed. She'd tamed me but unleashed me. She'd cured me but ruined me. How could I compete with a woman who had the power to kill me if anything ever happened to her?

I paced away, digging at my pounding head. "That's the fucking thing. I want you pregnant, Tess. I want a child with you. But I hate the thought of you in pain. I already want to slaughter the kid for hurting you in childbirth. If I can't handle that shit now, how the fuck will I handle it when it happens?"

If it ever happens.

Tess gathered the sheet and scrambled off the bed. The white simplicity looked like a shroud around her delicious shoulders. "Tell me what you want, Q. You can't have it both ways. You want me pregnant…fine. We'll work together to make it happen. You don't want me pregnant? Also, fine. We can adopt or do any other number of things. You just need to be honest about what you need."

What did I need?

I didn't fucking know.

But I knew what I needed to do. "I want your child. *Our* child. I do enough for orphans and survivors of the world. I've dedicated my life to supporting those in need and abandoned. Is it so wrong of me to want something of my own?" Rage howled in my chest. I had everything I could ever want. I was being so damn selfish. But the beast inside craved ownership on this one thing. I didn't want to settle. If that made me an asshole, then so be it.

I already knew I was one.

My hands shook as I muttered, "I don't want to adopt. That isn't what this is about."

Tess nodded. "Okay, I get that." She looked at the carpet, hugging the sheet tighter. "In that case, we should go and get checked out. Make sure we're both fit and able to get preg—"

I sliced my hand through the air. "No. No doctors or tests. Not until we have to. We give it a little longer before we consider that."

I couldn't stomach her being touched by a stranger or me being told I wasn't able to do this. If I was the problem…then it was my issue, and I would bear it on my own.

Tess scowled. "But you said I've been off contraception for two months. Perhaps it's a good time to see—"

"Two months is nothing. That damn chemical you injected yourself with should be almost gone."

"That damn chemical was what I thought we needed to have a happy marriage."

I snarled. "That was before, all right?"

Pinpricks of anger painted her cheeks. "I know, and I accept that. This is as scary for you as it is for me. We've gone from never discussing this to fighting about making it happen tomorrow." She sighed, doing her best to rid her frustration. "Q, these things take time. You just—you can't get stressed about it. And you can't impose stupid conditions on our sex life just because you think it makes you unworthy of becoming a father."

I laughed coldly. "That condition is non-negotiable." Moving toward her, I seethed. "I'm not going to touch you like I did last night. Got it? Not because it makes me unworthy. But because you ought to be fucking adored rather than cut by some sick fuck with issues. "

Her eyebrow rose. "Take that back. You aren't that at all."

"You don't know what goes on inside my head, Tess."

"So you said last night. But I don't need to. I know you, Q. And I love you." She grabbed my balled fist, holding on as I tried to shake her off. "Besides, I think you're misunderstanding how making a baby works." She giggled softly, doing her best to rid the argument brewing. "You have to do a lot more of what we did last night to make that happen."

I paced away, cursing the heat in my skin from her touch and the beg in my cock to do exactly what I just vowed I wouldn't. I wanted to hurt her constantly. My thoughts were dripping with black. But there was also light in there, too. A light that hadn't existed until Tess.

I would do everything in my power to make that light win over the blackness inside. If I couldn't keep her safe from me now, how the hell would I be able to keep any child of ours protected?

Tess chased me, wrapping her arms around me again and kissing my sparrow tattoo. "Promise me you'll keep doing what we have since we met. It's us. Ours. You can't stop it."

"Wrong." I stepped back again, breaking her hold. I couldn't have her touch me while we fought. I didn't trust myself not to lash out in anger or grab her to make violent love to her. "What we did—what we do—it's the reason you can't get pregnant."

"Not this again." She moaned. "Q…it's not. Don't torture yourself—"

"I'm not torturing myself. Or you for the considerable future. From now on…we're strictly vanilla."

"Vanilla?" Her eyes popped wide. "Oh, no. No way. Don't

you *dare* do that to me, Q."

"Do you think I want that, either?" The idea was abhorrent to the madness living inside me. The thought of chaste kisses and no passion. The idea of simple positions with no toys. It well and truly muzzled me. But it was what had to happen. I wasn't worthy of getting her pregnant. But if I treated her better, perhaps I would be. "I won't change my mind, Tess."

Challenge fired in her gaze. "You want to bet?"

"I want you to obey." Wrapping dangerous arms around her, I forced myself for the first time to touch her as if she'd break. I hugged her gently rather than fiercely. I kissed her sweetly rather than viciously, and I made a vow to keep myself caged until she was pregnant.

And then...once she was? Once she swelled with my unborn baby, would I be allowed to ruin her again?

Fuck, no.

Fear cloaked me. This was it. I'd had her to myself for so many precious years. I'd done everything I wanted, all that I pleased. If only that had remained enough for me. Because now I would turn my *esclave* from my naughty, kinky wife into the mother of my child.

I could never touch her the way I wanted again.

Is it worth destroying what you have?

I had no answer to that.

I had no idea what I needed or wanted anymore, and it pissed me off.

I supposed I'd have to remain chained to keep her safe because no way in fucking hell would I hurt her while she carried our unborn son or daughter.

I shivered at those two titles.

Me.

With a son or daughter.

It was laughable. Suicidal.

But it was also what I wanted most in the motherfucking world.

Moving with her in my embrace, I murmured, "Let's go for a shower together. A nice vanilla shower."

Tess frowned. "You can't be serious."

"Oh, I'm deadly serious. And nothing you can say will tempt me otherwise."

She grumbled but obeyed as I pulled her gently toward the bathroom. "We'll see about that, *maître*. I give you a day before you snap."

I hated her pessimism and my internal agreement.

Not taking her the way I needed would be the hardest damn thing I'd ever done.

But I was committed.

And I wouldn't falter.

"I love you, Tess. And that is why I'm doing this."

As I stripped her of the bed sheet and turned on the shower where I'd broken her awful memories of rape and kidnapping, I refused to think about what my self-imposed damnation would do to her. She was as twisted as me. Sex had always been our safe place. Now, it was unknown. Forbidden.

But for this to work, we would have to give up a piece of ourselves.

For however long we needed.

I'D LIKE TO say Q changed his mind the second we stepped into the shower together. I'd love to say he snapped and shoved me against the tiles like the monster he was.

But he didn't.

He washed me with all the reverence and care in the world.

He kissed me with barely any tongue.

And when he slid inside me, he wasn't fully hard, and I wasn't fully wet.

We weren't hardwired for simple pleasures.

We fought because we needed that extra level of sensation. And he'd just taken it away.

* * * * *

That afternoon, when he came home from work, I waited to see how long his self-imposed vanilla would last. I did my best to entice him after we crawled into bed, but he only hugged me until I unwillingly went to sleep.

For a week, that was the norm.

Q would take me every morning when we were both still sleep-hazy and not entirely coherent. He'd fill me after touching me with tormenting, teasing, and in no way satisfying strokes. He'd make me ready but not molten. And he'd come deep inside me, but it strained him. I could tell the struggle it was for him to orgasm without making me gasp and beg.

He needed my pain to get off. And without it, we both struggled to connect.

After we'd finished, I saw a pinprick of blood on the covers from where he'd dug his fingers into his palms so hard he'd broken the skin, seeking that sliver of wrongness to finish.

I didn't let him see the tears in my eyes at how much that hurt or how destroyed I was that he hadn't turned to me like he always had, finding salvation in my agony and screams.

Instead of being open and loving, we became closed off and uncertain.

And every day was worse than the last.

* * * * *

A week turned to a fortnight.

A fortnight turned to a month.

For the first time in our marriage, I didn't look forward to sex with my delectable husband. It became an obligation. Boring. And it was a chore to open my legs while in missionary style and allow a few shallow thrusts before my seriously twisted but imprisoned monster came inside me.

If this was what it took to get pregnant…then I didn't know how much longer I could stand it.

My thoughts turned nasty toward whatever child we would conceive. Yes, I wanted a family with Q. I wanted to share him with his children. But I also didn't want to lose him in order to gain them.

I was selfish where my *maître* was concerned. And if I couldn't have him, then I didn't want anything else.

Thoughts that Q might be sterile crossed my mind. After all, we had a very active sex life. Yes, I'd been on contraception injections for a long time, but that would've been out of my system by now…surely?

This was wrong.

Despicable.

This *hurt*.

I missed him. I missed *us*.

I'd been an understanding wife. After those first few

weeks of doing what I could to get him to break with no luck, I gave up. I didn't want to be the cause of more strife for him but I also didn't hide the agony of my sacrifice.

Q knew I was unhappy.

Shit, he was unhappy. Dreadfully so.

We were playing a treacherous game. Vanilla was supposed to be bland and non-lethal. But to us…it had the power to dismantle our marriage and shatter all that we loved.

On the fifth week, when three days had gone by and Q hadn't touched me, I ignored his requests not to involve doctors. I couldn't stand much more of this, and I wanted to know either way. I couldn't test Q without him knowing, but I could test myself.

I couldn't trust Franco to drive me to the clinic, so I enlisted the help of Suzette. She'd seen me growing bored and the change in Q as weeks crept onward. She'd been my shoulder to moan and fret on, understanding my frustration with Q's pigheadedness.

No wonder he was able to find me the second time I was kidnapped. His sheer mindedness when he made a decision was unarguable.

Q did this to protect me. However, without me as his outlet he started taking his violence out on his employees. Barking orders, firing a few for minor misconduct, and unable to keep his mask on in society. His life was no longer happy, and he refused to let me reach him.

It was time for drastic measures.

Pretending we were going to Paris to shop, Suzette and I arranged a day to take the high-speed train to the appointment I'd made in secret.

I'd researched online for the best fertility clinic and sneakily made a booking three days ago.

Suzette and I didn't talk much on the train, and for a second, I pretended life was simple and I was an architectural student again, heading into the city with a girlfriend for lunch, rather than the truth that I was a complicated woman terribly missing her harsh master.

After hailing a cab, we arrived at the address. Silently, we entered the building where I filled in a few forms and sat in a plush recliner beside Suzette until I was called into the doctor's office.

Giving me an encouraging smile, Suzette waited patiently in the sleek waiting room.

My hands shook as I entered the doctor's suite and closed the door.

"Hello, Mrs. Mercer."

I'd become so used to French accents, I did a double take finding this woman was English. I didn't often feel like a stranger in this city, but hearing another foreigner made me a little wistful.

Facing the medical practitioner, I put my future happiness in her hands.

Dr. Fellows smiled as my heels clicked on her white tiled floor. The air of the room was entirely clinical with no personality whatsoever.

I nodded. "Hello."

She wasn't old but she wasn't young, either. I guessed late forties. Blonde hair tucked neatly into a bun while the lashings of mascara and pink lipstick made her pretty but professional.

Had she had children of her own? Had she ever gone through this stress of a stubborn husband and floundering sex-life?

Pointing at a chair beside her desk, she said, "So, from our very brief conversation online, I hear you're trying to get pregnant but struggling?"

Sinking onto the seat, I nodded again. "Yes, my husband and I have been trying, but we're not succeeding. The chore of having sex just to get pregnant is wearing on me and I want to know either way." I didn't tell her why I wanted my monster back. Why I was alone without him and desperate for what we used to have. Five weeks was too long not to connect in the way we needed.

Dr. Fellows scanned her computer, pulling up information on who knew what. "Okay, well we'll start with a full examination and then we'll have a chat. How about that?"

My hackles rose.

I was happy for her to prod my body but not my mind. Until Q, I was an outcast and uncommon. No one could understand the way I was hardwired. That wouldn't have changed now I was older. When I was younger, I had no courage to be open about who I truly was. Now, I was wiser, and I didn't give a rat's ass what other people thought about me. But blatantly telling this stranger that I missed my husband hitting me and drawing blood? That would mostly cause me to be shipped off to a nunnery and locked up for my safety.

I'd been locked up far too often in my past by assholes who'd tried to break me. I wouldn't let it happen again. Then again, this woman was nothing compared to what I'd endured.

A flicker of abusive men and awful drug-sickness filled my mind.

My throat closed.

Oh my God, maybe I'm the reason why I can't get pregnant?

Perhaps the rape I'd endured and the drugs I'd been fed had ruined me? Maybe the kicks to my stomach and damage of my physical form had decimated any hope of being able to carry a healthy baby for Q.

I couldn't believe I hadn't thought about it before. Why hadn't I considered it?

Because you're so worried about Q thinking it's his fault that he's got you convinced.

Being away from him for the first time in months allowed me to think clearer. What if this *was* all my fault?

"Are you okay? What are you thinking about?" Dr. Fellows patted my hand. "You went white just now."

Pulling my hand from hers, I smiled weakly. "I'm okay. Just a thought, that's all."

"About your past and what might be obstructing your chances at getting pregnant?"

I looked at my entwined fingers in my lap. The designer jeans and silver oversized jumper with Hermes scarf labeled me as well off and content, but my fingernails were bitten from the malicious uncertainty of the past few weeks. "A little."

"Do you want to talk about it?"

"Not really."

"What makes you think you've done something to affect your chances?"

I swallowed a caustic laugh. "I have a few things that could."

Dr. Fellows narrowed her eyes. "You're not obligated to tell me, but everything you do will help me make an accurate diagnosis. Don't be afraid of it leaving this room. I'm bound by client confidentiality, and even if I wasn't, I don't believe in gossip." She smiled. "You can trust me, Mrs. Mercer."

Mrs. Mercer.

I was no longer Tess.

I could be honest with this woman, and she wouldn't judge me.

Forcing courage into my voice, I looked up. "A few years ago, I was kidnapped, sold into slavery, and bought." *By the man I married and the best beast I know.* "In a separate incident, I was raped and kidnapped, only to be fed drugs as a way of control and beaten daily."

The doctor sucked in a harsh breath. "And you underwent medical help for these incidences?"

"Yes." Q's personal physician. I'd had good care but perhaps not the gynecological care I needed. "However, I'm not sure if all bases were covered."

The doctor stood up, brisk efficiency surrounded her rather than judgment. "In that case, no time like the present. Let's get you on the table and begin." As she patted the gurney and plastic coverings waiting for me to strip and bare everything to this woman, she added, "I promise you we'll find the answers. We'll put your mind at rest, and I'll help you deal with whatever we find once we get the results. Okay?"

All my life, I hadn't latched onto people. I'd been disciplined by parents and a sibling who didn't want me. I'd learned to rely on myself and not others. Q had made me lean on him, and I'd found a sisterhood in Suzette, but I suddenly wanted to grab this stranger in a huge hug and thank her.

Fighting the urge, I nodded. "Okay."

Feeling stronger and more confident, I didn't hesitate. Shrugging out of my clothes, I submitted to the consultation.

The first part of the examination went fine. Dr. Fellows drew blood. Inspected my vitals and kept all opinions from her face as she noticed the brand on my neck and the tattoos on my wrist and finger.

Thank God, I didn't come here a few weeks ago when the bruises and cuts from Q's drunken night still marked me. She might've reported me to the women's shelter and had the police investigate.

I snuffed a small smile.

I'd already set the cops onto Q and look how that turned out. Or at least, Brax had. Q had the police in his pocket because he was a goddamn saint with what he did.

Why couldn't he see that?

He was so much better than what he believed.

As the exam grew more invasive, I trembled, fighting residual memories that I thought I'd worked through so many years ago. Having Q between my legs was welcome. Having his teeth in my flesh and his hand print on my ass was no better joy. But having a woman spread me open for the vaginal examination brought fleeting images of Mexico, Leather Jacket, and the rape before Q killed the man and rescued me.

"Are you okay?" Dr. Fellows murmured as I shook and clutched the plastic sheet as she finished the Pap smear.

Biting my lip, I kept my eyes locked on the ceiling. "Uh-huh."

Sealing the cotton swab and pulling off rubber gloves, she said, "You can get dressed now. All done." Pushing back on her wheeled chair, she shot to her desk and placed my swab in an outgoing tray and typed something on her computer.

I quickly pulled up my knickers and jeans before fluffing my hair and joining her. "How long will it take to know what's wrong with me?"

"That's the incorrect mindset to have. There is nothing wrong with you, Mrs. Mercer." Softening her voice, she added, "A few days for the blood-work to come in. However, in the physical examination, I didn't see anything wrong." Holding up a plastic cup, she grinned. "Whoops. Almost forgot. Go pee, please. I'll do a final test before you leave."

Eww.

Dutifully, I took the little container and left her office to head to the ladies' room at the end of the corridor. After doing what I needed, I returned and tried to fight my embarrassment at handing over such a disgusting thing.

Slipping more gloves on, Dr. Fellows pulled out a litmus stick and a few other medical paraphernalia and performed the tests right in front of me.

I watched silently.

Growing up, I hadn't had much experience with doctors. I rarely got sick, and if I did, my parents didn't bother taking me to the GP. I wasn't sure if I liked having someone looking after me or uncomfortable to be so investigated.

While waiting for whatever tests to show results, Dr. Fellows typed up a script and handed it to me. "Here are a few vitamins to boost your system to better enable your system to get pregnant. I'll also refer you to a family planning expert do discuss fertility options if it comes to that."

"Thanks."

Her eyes drifted to the test. Her face tightened as a smile lifted her lips. "Mrs. Mercer...I have some news for you."

"Already?" I strained my neck, trying to see what she did. "What is it? Am I sterile? It's me, isn't it? I'm missing something. Well, at least Q can stop beating himself up about it." *And start beating me again.* "I'm so sorry for wasting your time. Thanks for your help."

Standing, I trembled with a mixture of relief to finally have an answer and terrible sadness that I would never be a mother. I would never be able to give Q what he suddenly desperately wanted.

Dr. Fellows laughed. "Don't jump to conclusions. I hadn't finished." Pointing at the chair, she commanded, "Please, sit. You might need to when I tell you."

"Tell me what?"

She cocked her chin at the chair, waiting until I sank back down again. "It gives me great pleasure to be the first to tell you this, Mrs. Mercer."

Anticipation scraped along my skin as Dr. Fellows held up a stick with two blue lines. "You're pregnant."

* * * * *

"So? How did it go?" Suzette asked after we'd walked the streets of Paris in silence for half an hour.

How did it go?

I was pregnant.

I'm pregnant.

Q was right. It was our violent lovemaking stopping us.

No, that's wrong.

Once Dr. Fellows recorded the positive test, she reexamined me, doing a vaginal ultrasound and taking educated guesses.

Five to six weeks.

Not four weeks or one week.

And what had we done five weeks ago?

Q had come home obliterated and gone rogue. He'd strangled me, bit me, fucked me like the animal he was. And I'd adored every delicious debased second.

He'd knocked me up while doing the one thing he thought was stopping me from getting pregnant. The past few weeks of tame vanilla had been for nothing. He'd ruined our happy coexistence all because of some pigheaded idiocy.

Damn man.

My heart growled all while it bubbled with happiness.

Suzette pinched my forearm. "Are you going to tell me? Either you're dying, and that's why you can't tell me or..." Her face lit up. "Oh, my God. Are you?" She yanked me to a stop on the streets of Paris. "You're pregnant?"

Tears swam in my eyes, making her dance. "I—I—"

"Oh, you are. You *are!*" She grabbed me in a massive hug. "Wow, this is...wait until Q knows. Oh my God, Tess, he was right. What he's done the past few weeks." Her face fell. She knew how tame my love life had become. And I understood her conclusion. "This will kill him. He'll never touch you how you want again. He'll think everything he needs is even more wrong." She squeezed my hand in consolation. "I'm sorry, *mon amie.*"

My face split into a large smile. "I'm not. He had it wrong."

He was wrong when he said it was his fault. Wrong that his savage love meant he wasn't a worthy father.

I'd proven him otherwise and couldn't wait to tell him.

And this time, I'd win and get my beast back.

She frowned. "What?"

"Five weeks, Suzette. I'm five or six weeks pregnant. I'm going to say five because it fits better with my story." I laughed. "What happened five weeks ago?"

Her forehead furrowed, doing her best to think back that far. "Um..." She shrugged. "No idea."

"Q came home drunk..."

Realisation entered her gaze. "Oh...you guys left the pool room in a mess. Clothes everywhere...your sliced-up yoga band. When I went in the next day, it looked like a water polo fight had happened in there."

"Exactly." Smugness filled me. "The one night he thought he was hurting me so he could protect me from himself was the night he got exactly what he wanted."

Happiness blossomed on her face. "So... the past few weeks of boringness are over?"

I took her hand; full of ideas of how I would tell Q and

what I would make him do to me to make up for the past few weeks. "They are. And thank God for that."

Happiness I'd never felt before blossomed.

I'm pregnant!

With Q's child.

We're a family.

I'd been pregnant for weeks and not known.

According to Dr. Fellows, my system had become fertile far sooner than most women who'd been on the injection. She said the blood-work would give an exact conception date but anywhere from seven to five weeks was a good guestimate. It was great news all around. For me, Q, and our marriage.

There wouldn't have to be tests or consultations. We'd conceived naturally, and Q could finally have something of his very own.

Including me, of course.

The healthy meals Mrs. Sucre had plied us with had given my body a great foundation to form our little monster. And I no longer had to bore myself stupid with vanilla.

I was surprised Q hadn't noticed anything different about me.

Then again, I hadn't noticed, and I was the one changing. Q wasn't that observant when it came to my time of the month. He wasn't a husband to count my days and inform me that any second now I could start bleeding. So my secret would be all the more precious to share.

"I'm the first to know," Suzette said. "I'm honoured."

"Second." I smiled. "I was the first. Now, go home. I'm going to stay and plan something in order to tell Q. I'll be safe."

"Can I tell Mrs. Sucre?" Suzette hugged herself. "She'll burst into tears, I guarantee it. Our master is finally getting a family."

I shook my head. "He's always had a family…you guys."

Suzette blushed.

Clapping my hands, my head raced with ideas for tonight. "Anyway, hold the secret...for now. I want to tell."

"Of course. I wouldn't dare." Suzette pecked my cheek. "Let me know if you need any help with tonight."

"I won't. I'll call Q and tell him I'm alone in Paris. He'll come running."

Unfortunately, today was Monday, and that meant a big day at work, even though Q was supposed to hand most of the operation to Frederick. He was tied to his business, and I doubted he'd ever be totally free.

A small wash of nausea rolled through me, reminding me I was lucky to avoid morning sickness up till now. When would that start? Would I have a hard pregnancy or easy?

So many questions and so much to learn.

But Q would be there with me every step.

"WHERE THE FUCK are you?"

Her voice echoed down the line. "Don't have a heart attack, Q."

I'd worry about my heart while she worried about her backside because once I caught her, she'd be punished. Hard.

You're not allowed to touch her like that.

An oath was an oath, no matter how fucking difficult it was to keep. "I asked you a question, Tess. Where abouts in goddamn Paris are you?"

"I'm safe if that's what you're asking. I had an errand to run."

Tess never went to Paris without telling me first. She was safe now after I'd slaughtered the bastards from her past, but I never relaxed. Shadows and devils lurked everywhere, and Tess was such an enticement. I hated the fact she'd gone on the train without me. I loathed that she'd enlisted Suzette's care rather than my own.

We'd had a few problems the last few weeks.

But I was still her fucking husband.

My body vibrated with rage as I clutched the phone. "Why the hell would you do that?"

"I had my reasons." Traffic noise honked in the distance. "I'll tell you but only face to face. I'm calling to see if you want to meet here. Have the night with me in the city?"

I rubbed a hand over my eyes. My desk was littered with business mergers and recent acquisitions along with expanding more heavily into the orphanage and homeless children charity. I had so much on my plate; my mind had been foggy for weeks. Ever since I started treating Tess with kid gloves, I hadn't been able to concentrate.

For the first time since welcoming her into my bed, I wanted to orgasm while away from her. I was tempted to lock myself in the bathroom and squeeze my cock while fantasizing about what I used to do to her. It killed me to touch her so gently. And getting hard while stroking her rather than biting her was a non-winnable mission.

I loved her. I found her beyond attractive. But not being able to give in to the madness inside screwed me up.

"You want a night in Paris?" My voice dropped to a growl. Images of kinky pain, pressed against the hotel window, and furious sex in a foreign bed filled my mind.

Christ, I want to.

"I can't." If I did, I'd fuck her rather than make love to her. I'd hurt her. I'd ruin everything that we'd tried to make. I'd given myself two months since the night in the pool. If she wasn't knocked up by then, I would submit to doctor's tests and opinions. I had three more weeks before that happened. I wouldn't jeopardize it by giving in to what I wanted more than anything. "I have too much work to do."

The lie percolated in my chest when what I really wanted to say was *you're not safe with me.* Not right now.

Tess dropped her voice. "Too bad, *maître.* I've already reserved the pent-house at the Ritz. I'll be there all night. It's your call if you want to join me. Either way, I'm not coming home."

Ferocity filtered into my muscles, shooting me upward from my desk chair. "*Esclave,* don't you dare threaten—"

The phone call cut off, hanging dead in my hand.

Fuck!

Everything inside wanted to teach her a goddamn lesson.

Remind her that she couldn't get away with such rebellion. But in order to punish her, I had to hurt her, and I wouldn't do that. Not anymore.

Resentment billowed. I wanted to be furious at Tess, but mainly, I directed it at myself. Every day of my existence, I prided myself on having ultimate control over my darkness and fucked-up desires. However, Tess had shredded my restraint, given me freedom to be who I truly was, and then made me fall in love knowing she loved me back.

She'd given me so much.

And I was the one who'd changed the rules between us. I was the one who'd hurt her by pulling away. And I didn't know how to fix it.

I wanted her to carry our future. I wanted to keep her safe like I'd always done. Was that so bad? Didn't the gift of what we *could* have outweigh the intolerable payment in our present?

She'd kept my beast alive and in control of me. And now that I'd shackled that part, she acted as if I'd broken something perfect between us.

Daily, she tried to undermine my control, doing her best to coerce me into letting go. She couldn't be trusted anymore, and if I couldn't trust her, how the hell could I trust myself?

I wanted more. I wanted to drive deep inside her and do what I hadn't been able to do. That animalistic craving of making her pregnant consumed my thoughts. She made me feel less like a man. Unworthy. Not the man I knew. And I hated it.

If she wanted to talk about our issues on unknown territory in Paris, then fine.

Maybe it was for the best.

Pressing the intercom to my secretary outside, I snarled, "Call the helicopter. *Je veux être au Ritz immédiatement.*" I want to be at the Ritz immediately.

* * * * *

"Welcome to the Ritz, Mr. Mercer."

My temper was about to snap. I couldn't be around anyone other than my wife. And even then, I needed a room between us, so I didn't raise my hand in discipline. What if she'd been taken from me again? What if any number of things happened while I was at work and not able to protect her?

Damn her.

Fuck her.

She was going to get a spanking. Multiple. Screw my vow to keep her safe from me.

"The key to the presidential suite."

The manager handed it over, well trained in recognizing the needs of clients and knowing when to shut the hell up. The moment the key hit my palm, I strode toward the bank of elevators and the private one reserved for the suite on the top floor.

Stepping inside the silver box, I punched the button to ascend.

I had no luggage. No belongings.

But I didn't need anything because my wife was waiting for me and I would cart her home even if it meant the public saw me dragging her by her hair.

I wouldn't tolerate such things.

Not when it made me so fucking worried about her.

The elevator opened. I stormed out, slamming the keycard into the ornate double-breasted door, and entering the suite.

Stalking through the opulent space with marbled living room, kitchen, and games room, I found Tess coming out of the bathroom.

A towel wrapped around her head showed off her swan neck with the silvery brand. Her willowy body was covered with an oversized hotel towel, hiding so much of her from view.

The moment her eyes met mine, she froze. "Wow, that was fast."

Instead of doing what I wanted—bolting toward her and slamming her on the bed—I took a step back, locking my hands on the doorjamb of the bedroom. "You're coming home with me. Now."

Her chin tilted. "No, I'm not. I want to spend the night with you here. I miss you, Q. I want what we used to share." Her fingers went to the towel on her head, unwrapping it and letting damp blonde curls cascade over her milky skin. Boldly, she tugged at the knot on her chest, stepping from the second towel and revealing her stunningly naked figure.

My fingernails stabbed into the doorframe, holding me back with strained willpower. "Tess, put some fucking clothes on."

Her lips curved. "Make me."

"I'm not coming near you."

"Why?"

"You know why."

Her gaze hooded as she stepped toward me, bringing temptation directly to my door. "I do know why and I want it. I want it so much, Q. I need you. Please, we both know vanilla isn't working. It's not satisfying either of us."

"Reste loin." Stay away.

Tess ignored me. Her hands landed on my belt, quickly undoing it and yanking it from the belt loops.

I saw red. I saw pleasure. I saw damnation.

"Tess…"

"Yes, *maître.*"

"Get away from me."

Instead of obeying, she kneeled at my feet, holding my belt in outstretched hands. "Make me."

Oh, my fucking God.

I swayed as the animal inside sprang and snarled, demanding to maul her and take what I'd wanted to take for weeks.

My teeth almost cracked I clenched so hard. "I can't."

"You can." Her eyes narrowed with grey-blue fire. "And do you know why?"

I didn't reply, focusing too much on fighting her temptation.

"Because that night five weeks ago, when you took me

drunk and bare, was the night you achieved what you wanted. The past month of mollycoddling and chaste kisses have been for nothing."

I froze.

I couldn't speak.

But Tess didn't need prompting. Swatting her own thigh with my belt, I hissed at the pink welt left on her perfect skin. "I have a secret."

My frustration deepened as she ran the belt between her thighs. "I've been keeping something from you."

The insane need to punish her for such a thing overtook me. I struggled to bite the words. "What? What have you been keeping secret?"

Was she sick?

Unhappy?

Because right now, I was both those things. Sick with want and desperately unhappy for not having the freedom I adored between us.

She smiled coyly. "I'm fine. However, I do have some information you might want to know."

I trembled in place. "Spit it out, Tess."

Raising her eyebrow, she whispered, "I'm pregnant."

My knees gave out, depositing me before her. "*What* did you just say?"

Her lips stretched into a blinding smile. "You knocked me up when you let yourself fully go. That was what I needed. What *we* needed. We come alive when we're together with no cages or locks between us."

I shook my head. "Again. Tell me again."

Her gaze melted with adoration. "I'm pregnant."

"*Pregnant?*" I couldn't compute. "Pregnant...as in...*pregnant?*"

She nodded with a wide smile. "And for our child's sake, I hope it's a boy."

I couldn't...I didn't believe her. "You're—you're—"

Tess touched my cheek with all the love in the world.

"Congratulations, Q. You're going to be a father."

"And you think it's a boy?"

"No, I don't know what it is yet. I just hope it is so you don't die of a heart attack trying to protect a daughter. You don't need to go to war to protect a baby girl just yet." She chuckled softly. "Maybe once you've learned to relax a bit more…then we could try for a daughter."

First, she told me she was pregnant. The one thing I wanted more than anything else. Then, she said she wanted more with me. A family of our own. *Multiple* children.

I couldn't do it.

Grabbing her, I lashed my arms around her naked form. My lips landed on her throat as I kissed and nipped and thanked her.

"Fuck, is this true?"

She giggled. "Yes, it's true."

I wasn't a man who cried. I'd seen a lot in my life and never shed a tear.

No, that wasn't right.

I'd let a few escape when Tess had strapped me to the bed, and I screamed for mercy before she killed me. Even now, the faint scars from that day still graced my face and body.

I'd given Tess what she needed to break her past and finally be free. And she'd just done exactly the same for me.

We'd both learned so much from each other.

And soon, we would learn so much more.

But that was life.

A never-ceasing evolution to our perfect happiness.

My gaze landed on her flat stomach. "How can you be pregnant? You're not showing."

"I'm too early to show. And I'm pregnant because of the usual way." Unable to stop her good mood, she added, "I booked a private meeting with a gynecologist here in Paris. I was going out of my mind with your incessant need not to touch me. I needed to know either way."

She shrugged, growing shy. "The test showed I'm

pregnant. And the timeline puts conception at that night in the pool, or even a couple weeks earlier." She raised my belt once again. "So you see, Q. You have no reason not to be yourself. Come back to me. I'm begging you."

I reared back. "You expect that, just because you're pregnant, I'm going to hurt you again? Fuck, I'm never going to touch you again. We'll be celibate for nine months until you deliver safely, and even then I'll treat you like the queen you are. Our past is done. We've been kidding ourselves by thinking that's normal. It's not normal. *I'm* not normal. I can't keep letting that part of myself free when it's so fucking wrong." My voice threatened with a growl as both facets of myself waged war.

Tess bared her teeth. "If you do that. If you stop being the man and monster I married, then we won't last. Being pregnant won't matter."

Ice water replaced my blood. "What the fuck are you saying?"

"I'm saying be the man I want. Hurt me. It's not a request. I need it just like you do. This is *our* normal. The rest isn't. Don't ruin us because of some stupid ideal to conform. If you do that, Q, we'll lose each other and grow apart. Is that what you want? For our marriage to fail?"

Of course, I didn't want that.

She needed to wash her mouth out with soap for ever suggesting such a thing.

My eyes fell on the hotel property, judging and dispelling each item in terms of punishment capabilities. I wanted a magazine to roll or a lamp cord to tie. Or even a hard covered book to spank my naughty, stubborn wife.

Anything would do.

I squeezed my eyes. But I promised I wouldn't touch her in such a way.

She's pregnant.

The knowledge trickled through me, growing in decibel with every heartbeat.

Pregnant.

Nothing was wrong with me. I'd achieved what I needed. And it'd happened the night I thought would be our last free time together.

What did that say about us?

That our bodies had reacted far more potently by giving into our baser desires or that it was merely an accident?

I hadn't come here looking to talk. I'd come here to drag my *esclave* home where I could keep her safe. But Tess stood proud and defiant, her hands on her flat stomach. "Do you want that, Q?"

Her voice wrenched through my tumbling thoughts. "Do I want what?"

Her eyes glassed with tears. "Our marriage to fail?"

Shit, I hadn't replied. My chest expanded with anger. "I can't comprehend how you can ask such a horrid thing."

"I ask because I honestly don't know." Clutching her stomach, she murmured, "Is having a child worth cutting us apart?"

My heart fucking froze. Was that what I'd been doing? Tearing us into pieces while trying to chase the one thing that wouldn't matter at all if I couldn't have Tess?

My breathing turned deep and thoughtful for the first time in weeks. I'd been living on adrenaline, forcing myself to touch her with barely any force, struggling to get it up when we slept together, finding more and more salvation in my work even though I couldn't clear my head from weeks of self-denial.

She's right.

Capturing her elbow, I whispered, "No. It's not. I'd rather have you over a thousand children. Over every wealth in the world."

Her body breathed a heavy sigh of relief. "I'm so happy to hear you say that." Her eyes turned smoky with intent. "Now that you agree with me. Now that you know you got your way and I'm carrying your child...perhaps you can give in to me again. Come home to me, *maître*."

My gut twisted with gratefulness. What a lucky bastard I was. My wife wanted me in all my complexities, and she'd given me what I'd dreamed of.

Did I want to hurt her like we did before?

Yes.

Did I want to bruise and mark?

Without a fucking doubt.

Did I want to lock her up for the next nine months away from the world and keep her safe?

More than anything.

I'd done my best at castrating the beast inside me, but I couldn't do such a thing on my own. And Tess wasn't willing to permit me. Tess wanted me, darkness and all. I had to stop fighting the inevitable and be myself again.

Tess's relief trickled into me. The permission to relax and stop fighting what made us *us* siphoned away my guilt and shame.

She sucked in a breath, recognizing my switch. Biting her lip, she moved toward me and rested her palm on my chest. "Welcome back, husband. I've missed you."

I stopped breathing as she linked her fingers with mine, guiding me toward the bed. Her naked body was flushed and scrubbed. Droplets from the shower sparkled in the pristine lights of the Ritz suite.

My eyes dropped to the red outline of my belt on her thigh. She'd done that herself, but I craved to be the one to mark her other leg. To create brilliant symmetry of ownership.

My cock leapt with fucking joy—knowing the self-imprisonment had finished. The rush. The thrill. Every step toward the bed shook me harder.

I struggled to breathe as Tess sank gracefully on the mattress. She never broke eye contact, clasping an emotional collar around my throat and forcing me to heel and obey. Her damp hair coiled around her throat, dancing around her collarbone like an intricate necklace.

She looked so young.

But glowed with something infinite.

She's pregnant.

I shuddered with joy.

With a soft sigh, she reclined against the sheets. "What are you going to do to me?"

My hands fisted.

That question was far too dangerous.

My hands shot to my shirt and trousers. Tearing them off, I threw them to the floor. My shoes were kicked off into hotel corners and my boxer-briefs were banished. The second I was naked, I towered over Tess and fisted my hard length.

Tess licked her bottom lip, her face filling with wanton invitation. "I love when you stand over me. Do you want my mouth?" She drew her index along her bottom lip. "Or do you want my pussy?" With all the seduction of a goddess, Tess spread her legs for me, her fingertips gliding down her toned body to play with her clit.

Her stomach showed no hint of pregnancy. No clue to holding my unborn child. But I had to believe that Tess would keep whatever baby she carried safe. She was strong enough to do that for me. For us.

Squeezing my cock, I ordered, "Get up."

Her gaze drifted down my chest, over sparrows and ink to latch onto my very hungry erection.

It jerked under her inspection, begging for her wet heat.

Her body moved like silk, rising from the starched white bedding to stand in front of me.

Goddammit, she was stunning.

I locked my muscles to stop from reaching for her.

I saw two women: the one I'd promised to fight and hurt. And the other I vowed to love and cherish. And now, she would be a third woman. A mother who I'd protect with every last fucking breath.

The desire started as a fireball in my gut—igniting my blood until my entire body set alight with furious lust.

I needed to take Tess ruthlessly and painfully. I needed to

remember who I truly was at heart. My arms banded around her. "I'm going to make you remember who I am, *mon coeur.*" My heart.

My mouth stole hers. Our naked bodies slammed together, our fingers clawing at delicate skin. Her lips opened, submitting to my tongue as I licked inside her. I groaned as she kissed me back. Her hands skated over me, dragging me forward as her nails scratched down my spine.

"Q—please—"

My lips latched harder onto hers, kissing so deep. I wanted to crawl into her soul and capture her forever. The monster inside—the one who I'd forced to lay dormant for weeks— roared back to life.

Control.

The sickly need slithered in my blood, whispering of violence.

I shook my head, dispelling the rapidly building darkness. I would let him play, but I wouldn't let him rule. Not now. Not ever. My darling *esclave* was pregnant. She could handle our fucked-up love, but she couldn't handle total annihilation.

My fingers crept up, latching around her throat. Her muscles worked hard as she swallowed.

"Do you like destroying me, Tess? Is that why you called me here to hurt you?" I ran my nose down her cheek, inhaling the scent of expensive hotel soap.

She squeaked as I spun her around, pressing her chest into the bed and keeping her ass locked against my aching cock. "Answer me."

"Yes…I love watching the battle inside you. Knowing that you'll give in if I push you hard enough."

I rocked into her. "And is this giving in?"

She smiled over her shoulder through tangled wet hair. "It's a start."

I loved her.

I adored her.

I didn't want to hurt her.

Lies.

I did want to hurt her.

And she wanted me to.

That was ultimate freedom.

Bending over her, I scattered kisses down her spine. There were no toys in the hotel. We hadn't come prepared. We weren't at home where any number of apparatus was available to us.

We would have to compromise and invent, but all I could think about was taking her the way I didn't often do. A way that would punish her and reward her.

Her eyes locked onto mine.

Tess had such power over me—power I'd never be free of.

"What are you thinking?" I asked, keeping my voice low.

Her thighs clenched. "I'm wondering what you're about to do and hoping you lose all control."

I bared my teeth, heart heating with irritation. "I may be a lot of things, Tess, but if you think I'm going to open my cage fully while you're pregnant…you don't know me very well."

She pouted. "But I thought—"

"You thought wrong." My lips twitched in a cool grin. "However, it doesn't mean I won't punish you in other ways."

"Face away." I motioned for her to look at the bed and not me.

Unwillingly, she obeyed.

Not seeing made her oversensitive body hum with uncertainty.

My hand tickled as I indulged in the call inside. I spanked her once, turning her cooling skin pink with punishment.

She groaned, rocking back, sandwiching her ass against my erection. "I need you."

My hands landed on her hips, grunting as she rocked harder. Dragging my fingers over her bare pussy, I growled. "Fuck. Will I ever get enough of you?"

"God, I hope not." Tess jerked as I positioned my cock at

her entrance. Normally, I'd play with her and tease, but after the incredible news of our future, I just needed to connect. Immediately.

A much-needed release throbbed in my blood.

"Q…yes, Q." Tess threw back her head as I slipped inside her. The heavenly warmth of my wife sheathing me sent my heartbeat colliding with my ribs. I entered her an inch at a time.

With each inch, I spanked her, slicing my hand right over her ass. Not holding back the force of the sexual punishment. The fact she hadn't been hit for weeks only made her skin bloom brighter.

Unable to stop myself, I did it again. Strike, thrust. Strike, thrust. Tess moaned beneath me, her legs shivering as I slid fully inside her.

"Q!" she breathed. "I need you so much."

My fingers dipped between her legs. Her ass hot with my hand prints against my lower belly. "You need me?"

She cried out as I smeared wetness around her clit. She pushed back, arching into my touch. "More than anything."

My balls tightened, already extra sensitive and desperate to come. "*Merde, esclave,* you're ruining me." Giving in, I grabbed her hips, propping her higher over the edge of the bed.

All thoughts of games flew away as I pulled out and thrust hard into my wife. My voice tangled in the air. "This is going to be fast and hard. Are you ready, Tess?"

She nodded breathlessly. "God, yes."

My nails imprinted crescent moons on her skin as I jerked her to meet me, deleting all space between us. I didn't hold back, shuddering with bliss as I broke her flesh, licking my lips at the hint of my *esclave*'s blood.

Fuck.

Rubbing my fingertips in the sticky crimson, I painted her spine with red, before wrapping my hands in her hair to wrench her head back. I didn't worry about hurting her scalp. I didn't fear the contorted way her body bowed as I plunged deep inside. All I cared about was being free with this woman who'd insanely married me.

Time lost all meaning as we fucked and reaffirmed how we felt for each other.

My hands never ceased—pinching, spanking, punishing, and petting.

Each strike Tess moaned.

Each sharply delivered pain Tess cried out with joy.

I was addicted to this woman.

My *pregnant* woman.

My orgasm didn't stay away, and I forced her high and fast so I could chase her into the darkness and come.

We both finished on a long groan, slamming back to earth.

As we came down from our sexual high, panting and laughing, tangled in each other's arms like we always would, I revoked my oath to never hurt her again. I'd never be so fucking stupid to try and be something I wasn't.

She'd reminded me not to be so stubborn. And I loved her so damn much.

As sweat dried on our skin and the small teeth marks I'd punctured in her skin scabbed over, Tess murmured, "You're going to be a father, Q."

Hugging her close, I kissed her so sweetly it bordered diabetic. But she accepted my questing tongue with a sweetness of her own. We'd sated our rage and could be gentle…for now. "You're going to make a wonderful mother."

"Only as long as you promise to stay with me and accept us once and for all."

I nuzzled her brand. "I promise."

It was the easiest promise I'd ever made. Acceptance. Funny how I'd run from it all my life and it was so easy to give in to it now.

I loved this woman to the galaxy and back.

I always would.

She was my wife.

My *esclave*.

And soon, we would have a family.

EPILOGUE

SIXTEEN MONTHS LATER

THERE WERE MANY moments in my life that I treasured.

The day I was sold to Q.

The day I returned to Q.

The day I married Q.

Every event included my husband because I hadn't truly lived until I met him. And now, I had one more.

Watching Q be a father to Abelino, Lino for short, was no greater achievement in my life. The French name meant bird and Q instilled in his son every lesson he'd learned so our child might never know firsthand the evil of the world.

Those first few weeks of not knowing the sex of our child had worn on me. I wasn't joking when I said Q wasn't ready for a daughter. When we finally had the ultrasound and confirmed it was a boy, I burst into tears.

Q's eyes had glassed too, proving he wasn't monstrous, after all.

My pregnancy had been easy, thanks to Q's constant monitoring and support. He'd given into my demands for a rough session only a couple of times while I was pregnant and never when I got close to delivering. However, vanilla was a cursed word and never permitted in our lives again. I could live without using the swinging sex chair or the cross in our bedroom every week. I could concede not being whipped with a cat o' nine tails until I wept for mercy every other day.

Because I had something better.

I had a husband who still bit, bled, and abused me. Only he became even more creative. Parts of my body he hadn't paid too much attention to suddenly became orgasm triggers for my overly sexed pregnant form. Toys that at first glance seemed innocent became sinfully naughty when used in the right way. He also became a master at torturing me with that blasted magic wand.

Not to mention, the gift I'd given him on our wedding night became more and more desired by both of us. Anal wasn't something we'd done often but while I was pregnant, Q took his role as protector seriously. He was happier taking my ass than my pussy, saying he didn't want to invade his son's safe cocoon.

It made no sense. But Q was a man. And men had strange conclusions.

Our lives had fallen into a happy agreement we both loved. We still argued. Still snuggled. Still had a lot of sex and a couple of months after delivering Lino with no complications, I found Q in his study to deliver the news that I was healed from giving birth.

That day...

Wow.

That day had been one of the best in all my days of sexual experience. Q had stocked up on new supplies while I'd fumbled through my last trimester and he was only too happy to try them out now I was unencumbered with his child.

In a nine hour session, Q orgasmed four times and I doubled him with eight. Lino had to be given a bottle by Suzette that night rather than my breast because I could barely lift my head from the blissful subspace I swam in.

A month after Lino was born, we travelled to the man who'd done Q's chest piece, Louis. There, Q had another bird added to his tattoo, only this one wrapped around his back, splaying its feathered wings over his shoulder blades. The ink was grey-blue for my eyes, and its claws held two ribbons floating behind it with my name and our son's.

For so long, Q decorated his body with mementos of helping others. And now, he'd been able to ink his future rather than his past. Solidifying our family into his flesh forever.

Not wanting to be left out, I asked for a tattoo of a family of sparrows flying over my arm in honour of Q, the wings he'd given me, and the children we would hopefully conceive in the future.

Bringing my thoughts back to the present, I smiled, utterly content in the sleepy afternoon.

Lino played on his stomach in the French sunshine beside me, surrounded by Courage and the other puppies who were now all full grown. The dark blue jumpsuit Lino wore set off his chubby skin and dark wispy hair. For a baby, he was beautiful and I saw so much of Q in his pale innocent eyes. There was no doubt these Mercer men would break me by being so handsome and incredible.

Courage broke away from Lino, depositing a saliva drenched tennis ball by my feet. "Again? Really?"

The black French bulldog barked, running in a circle. I'd lost count how many times I'd thrown this ratty thing but Lino loved it. He squealed every time one of his guard dogs barreled past, chasing such a silly thing.

Wrenching my arm back, I threw as hard I could. Courage took off, leaping over Lino and his pack mates in his rush.

Q came out of the house, a brilliant smile cracking his lips. He'd been working this morning but now he would take the afternoon off to spend with us.

Noticing me lounging on the deck chair, he kissed my head before scooping up our son and blowing kisses on his neck.

The squirmy form of his baby swelled my heart until I glowed with gratefulness and overwhelming love.

Q met my gaze, hugging Lino close. His body language promised an evening of debauchery while his face promised me everything that he was. He'd worshipped me before with his whips and chains but it was nothing to how he treated me now. How he watched me as if I were the very reason his heart beat. How he touched Lino with reverence reserved for only the holiest of things.

He was in love with me.

I would never ever take that for granted.

Holding out my hand, I clutched Lino's bare foot dangling from my husband's embrace. Q wrapped his warm fingers around my wrist, squeezing just enough to remind me I belonged to him.

I would always belong to him.

Ducking, his lips met mine in a sensual kiss. My heart pattered and my nipples tingled for a session with my master rather than provide nutrition for our son.

Murmuring into our kiss, Q said, "Every hour makes me love you more. Every year, every minute, every moment we spend together. Tess...you do more than complete me. You heal me. And I'll spend my entire life making sure you understand that."

He'd said such words before. But they never lost the depth of meaning or sincerity.

My reply was a similar echo but in no way lacking the love I held for him. "Every hour I fall harder for you. Every year, every minute, every moment we live side by side is the best minute of my existence. I love you, Q, and I'll dedicate every breath making sure you accept it."

Our eyes locked as we kissed again, pulling apart as Lino wriggled for space.

Our devotion reaffirmed, Q chuckled, bouncing the boy in his arms. The sun glistened behind him making him seem outwardly, a god fallen to earth to rescue and marry me.

Sighing happily, I hugged myself as Q placed Lino on the blanket, sitting beside him on the grass to tickle and play.

This.

This was what made every hardship we'd been through worthwhile.

We had so much.

We were so damn lucky.

Our charities were well and truly established, and the women recuperating in the house across our estate found it easier to regroup with the rescued animals we brought home from the shelters that were too damaged to be rehomed.

Somehow, we'd become a zoo as well as a convalescent, but together, the broken survivors mended each other.

And in the middle of this fortress of healing, sat my king. The man who made it all possible.

He rarely went into the office anymore, preferring to do all his work from home so he never missed a moment of Lino's upbringing. Just having him close to kiss or run a hand through his hair when I needed contact made all my dreams come true.

Suzette was a born nanny and loved keeping an eye on Lino if Q's beast demanded a mid-afternoon solstice or early evening reunion. And her and Franco had announced they were getting married next summer.

Life was ridiculously perfect, and for the first time, I didn't fear the future or suspect anything sinister might tear it all away.

We were happy.

We *deserved* to be happy.

We would remain happy for the rest of our lives.

Because I had my monster.

And he had me.

And together, we had everything.

THE END

ABOUT THE AUTHOR

Pepper Winters is a multiple New York Times, Wall Street Journal, and USA Today International Bestseller. She loves romance, star-crossed lovers, and anything to do with character connection. She strives to write a story that makes the reader crave what they shouldn't, and delivers tales with complex plots and unforgettable characters.

After chasing her dreams to become a full-time writer, Pepper has earned recognition with awards for best Dark Romance, best BDSM Series, and best Hero. She's a multiple #1 iBooks bestseller, along with #1 in Erotic Romance, Romantic Suspense, Contemporary, and Erotica Thriller. She's also honoured to wear the IndieReader Badge for being a Top 10 Indie Bestseller, and signed a two book deal with Hachette. Represented by Trident Media, her books have garnered foreign and audio interest and are currently being translated into numerous languages. They will be in available in bookstores worldwide.

She loves mail of any kind: **pepperwinters@gmail.com**
All other titles and updates can be found on her **Goodreads Page.**

PLAYLIST

(Tears of Tess, Quintessentially Q, Twisted Together combined into this Playlist)

Demons by Imagine Dragons
Bring Me Back To Life by Evanescence
Arms by Christina Perri
Dark Paradise by Lana Del Ray
Undisclosed Desires by Muse
Animal by Disturbed
ET by Katy Perry
Halo by Depeche Mode
Monster by Imagine Dragons
Coldplay by Magic
Never Tear Us Apart by INXS
Adore by Miley Cyrus
Broken by Lifehouse
Between the Raindrops by Lifehouse
Everything by Lifehouse
Breath of Life by Florence & the Machine
She is by The Fray
Love Don't Die by The Fray
End of Time by Lacuna Coil
Closer by Nine Inch Nails
The Lonely by Christina Perri
My Heart is Broke by Evanescence
Addicted to you by Avici
Marry the Night by Lady Gaga
Something I need by One Republic
Darkside by Kelly Clarkson
Hunter by 30STM
Monster by Rihanna & Dr Dre
Move like a Sinner by What Now
Deep Inside by Third Eye Blind

Everlong by Foo Fighters
My Immortal by Evanescence
Do What You Want by Lady Gaga
Pictures of You by The Cure
Closer by Nine Inch Nails
Dark Horse by Katy Perry
Cold by Crossfade
Die for You by Megan McCauley
My Last Breath by Evanescence
Moondust by Jaymes
Skyscraper by Demi Lavato

FIRST OFFICIAL SNEAK PEEK INTO #SUPERSECRETSERIES.

Cover, title, full blurb, and release information will be shared on my website and newsletter on the 3rd June 2016. Sign up to my Facebook Group HERE to join the cover reveal party with prizes and fun on the 3rd June.

A brand new Dark Romance Series starting July 2016. This new monstrous hero will rival even Jethro Hawk and Q Mercer.
Get ready for...
Elder Prest.

Copyright Pepper Winters 2016
Unedited, subject to change.
No copying permitted.

Teaser Blurb

Tasmin was killed on her 18th birthday.
She had everything planned out. A psychology degree, a mother who pushed her to greatness, and a future anyone would die for. But then her murderer saved her life, only to sell her into a totally different existence.

Elder went from penniless to stinking rich with one twist of fate. His lifetime of crime and shadows of thievery are behind him but no matter the power he now wields, it's not enough. He has an agenda to fulfil and he won't stop until it's complete.

But then they meet.
A beaten slave and a richly dressed thief.
Money is what guided their separate fates. Money is what brought them together. And money is ultimately what destroys them.
She's poor.
He's rich.
Together…they are bankrupt.

Prologue

FREEDOM.

Such a simple word.

For those who had it, it carried very little importance. But for those who didn't have it, it was the most precious, prized, and promised hope of all.

I supposed I was lucky to know what freedom felt like.

For eighteen years, I'd been free. Free to learn what I wanted, befriend who I liked, and flirt with boys who passed my rigorous criteria.

I was a simple girl with ideals and dreams, encouraged by society to believe nothing could hurt me, that I should strive for an excellent career, and no one could stop me. Rules would keep me safe, police would keep the monsters away, and I could remain innocent and naïve to the darkness of the world.

Freedom.

I had it.

But then I lost it.

Until the day he entered my cage.

Him with the black eyes and blacker soul.

The man who challenged my owner.

And set my imprisonment on an entirely different path.

Chapter One

DEAR DIARY,

No, that didn't sound right. Far too light-hearted for my tale.

Dear Universe,

Scratch that. Too grandiose.

To The Person Reading This.

Too vague.

To The Person I Wish Would Help Me.

That would get me in trouble. And I refused to sound weak. Not if these words were the only thing strangers would remember me by.

To...

Tapping the broken pencil against my temple, I did my best to focus. For weeks, I'd been confined like a zoo animal being acclimatised to its new world. I'd been fed, washed, and given medical attention from my rough arrival. I had a bed with sheets, a flushing toilet, and shampoo in the shower. I had the basics that all human and nonhuman life required.

But I wasn't living.

I was dying.

They just couldn't see it.

Wait...I know.

Inspiration struck as I came up with the perfect name to address this sad letter to. The title was the only right in this wrong, wrong new world.

To No One.

The moment the three words were pressed into my poor parchment, I couldn't stop the memories unfolding. My left hand shook as I kept the toilet tissue flat while my right flew, slowly transcribing my past.

I WAS EIGHTEEN when I died.

I remember the day better than any other in my short life. And I know you're rolling your eyes, saying it only happened three weeks ago, but believe me, I will never forget this. I know some people say certain events are forever imprinted on their psyche, and up until now, I haven't had anything stick in such a way. You see, No One, I guess you could've called me a brat. Some might even say I deserve this. No, that's a lie. No one would wish this on their worst enemy. But the fact remains, only you know I'm not dead. I'm alive and in this cell about to be sold to the highest bidder. I've been hurt, touched, violated in every sense but rape, and been stripped of everything I used to be.

But to my mother? I'm dead. I died. I vanished. Who knows if she'll ever truly find out what happened to me.

The scribbling of my pencil stopped.

My will to stay breathing had vanished. It'd taken them a while to break me. But they had. And now that they'd achieved their goal, I was nothing more than cargo waiting for the transaction to line their pockets with my sale.

I sucked in a ragged breath. For days, all I'd had for entertainment were my chaotic thoughts, awful memories, and overwhelming panic of what lay ahead of me. But that was until I found the chewed up, snapped in half pencil beneath the bed.

The find had been better than food or freedom; better because both of those things were minutely controlled by my traffickers. I had no power to sway the regimented arrival of breakfast and dinner nor the ability to halt the fact I was being sold like meat to the highest bidder.

I had no control over being alone in a tiny room that had once been a hotel suite before its premises were bought for more unsavoury stays. The towels were threadbare with the sigil of some long ago establishment and the carpet swirled with golds and bronze hinting the decor hadn't been updated since the seventies.

Was that how long the pencil had lurked beneath my bed? Were the bite marks on the wood given by a rowdy toddler waiting for its parents to stop fussing so they could explore a new city? Or had a maid lost it while tucking starched white sheets with military precision?

I'd never know.

But I liked to make up fantasises because I had nothing else to do. I spent my achingly long days going over every nook and cranny of my jail. They'd broken my spirit, washed away my fight, but they couldn't stop the determined urge inside me. The instinct everyone had—or at least, I *thought* everyone had.

I'd been alone for so long, I didn't know what the other girls I was processed with would do. Did they lie star-spread on the bed and wait for their future? Did they huddle in the corner and beg for their fathers to stop this nightmare? Or did they accept, because it was easier to accept than to fight?

Me? I ran my rubbed-raw fingertips over every wall, every crack, every painted up window frame. I crawled on my hands and knees, searching for something to help me. And by help me, I didn't know if I meant as a weapon to fight my way out or something to end my struggle before it truly began.

It'd taken me days to go over every square inch. But all I'd found was this half-mangled pencil. A gift. A treasure. The nub was almost down to the wood and I wouldn't have long before I had to find ways to sharpen my precious possession, but I'd worry about that another day. Just like I'd become a master at shoving aside my worries about everything else.

The one thing I didn't find was any paper. Not in the drawers of the beat-up desk or in the cupboard beneath the non-functioning television. The only apparatus I could write on was toilet-paper and the pencil wasn't too keen on that idea, tearing the soft tissue rather than imprinting its silvery lines.

Nevertheless, I was determined to leave some sort of note behind. Some piece of me that these bastards hadn't taken and never would.

Taking a deep breath, I shoved aside my current conditions and clutched the pencil harder. Glancing at the door to make sure I was alone (I had three hours before dinner was served through the hole in the wall), I spread out my square of toilet paper to make it tight and writable and continued with my note.

I wish I could say a monster killed me. That a terrible accident caused this. And I can say that…to a degree.

However, the real reason I'm dead and a new toy about to be sold is mainly because of my upbringing.

That poise and confidence my mother drilled into me? It didn't grant me in good stead for a profitable career or handsome husband. It pissed people off. I came across as stuck-up, know-it-all, and vain.

It made me a target.

I don't know if anyone will ever see this but you, No One, but if they do, I hope they forget what I'm about to admit. I'm an only daughter to a single parent. I love my mother. I do.

But if I ever survive what's about to happen to me and by some miracle I find freedom again, I'll keep this next part to myself when I account my time in purgatory.

I love my mother, but I hate her.

I miss my mother, but I never want to see her again.

I obeyed my mother, but I want to curse her for eternity.

She's the only one I can blame.

The one responsible for me becoming nothing more than a whore.

Sign up here to receive updates and be notified when this is released:

HERE

BOOK BLURBS BY PEPPER WINTERS

Complete Duology
Ruin & Rule (Pure Corruption MC #1)

"We met in a nightmare. The in-between world where time had no power over reason. We fell in love. We fell hard. But then we woke up. And it was over . . ."

Buy Now

***

Sin & Suffer (Pure Corruption MC #2)

"Some say the past is in the past. That vengeance will hurt both innocent and guilty. I never believed those lies."

Buy Now

****

Complete Trilogy
Tears of Tess (Monsters in the Dark #1)

"My life was complete. Happy, content, everything neat and perfect. Then it all changed. I was sold."

Buy Now

***

Quintessentially Q (Monsters in the Dark #2)

"All my life, I battled with the knowledge I was twisted… screwed up to want something so deliciously dark—wrong on so many levels. But then slave fifty-eight entered my world. Hissing, fighting, with a core of iron, she showed me an existence where two wrongs do make a right."

Buy Now

***

Twisted Together (Monsters in the Dark #3)

"After battling through hell, I brought my esclave back from the brink of ruin. I sacrificed everything—my heart, my mind, my very desires to bring her back to life. And for a while, I thought it broke me, that I'd never be the same. But slowly the beast is growing bolder, and it's finally time to show Tess how beautiful the dark can be."

Buy Now

****

Complete Series
Debt Inheritance (Indebted Series #1)
"I own you. I have the piece of paper to prove it. It's undeniable and unbreakable. You belong to me until you've paid off your debts."

Buy Now

***

First Debt (Indebted Series #2)
"You say I'll never own you. If I win—you willingly give me that right. You sign not only the debt agreement, but another—one that makes me your master until your last breath is taken. You do that, and I'll give you this."

Buy Now

***

Second Debt (Indebted #3)
"I tried to play a game. I tried to wield deceit as perfectly as the Hawks. But when I thought I was winning, I wasn't. Jethro isn't what he seems-- he's the master of duplicity. However, I refuse to let him annihilate me further."

Buy Now

***

Third Debt (Indebted #4)
"She healed me. She broke me. I set her free. But we are in this together. We will end this together. The rules of this ancient game can't be broken."

Buy Now

***

Fourth Debt (Indebted #5)

'We'd won. We'd cut through the lies and treachery and promised an alliance that would free us both. But even as we won, we lost. We didn't see what was coming. We didn't know we had to plan a resurrection."

Buy Now

***

Final Debt (Indebted #6)

"I'm in love with her, but it might not be enough to stop her from becoming the latest victim of the Debt Inheritance. I know who I am now. I know what I must do. We will be together--I just hope it's on Earth rather than in heaven."

Buy Now

***

Indebted Epilogue (Indebted #7)

INDEBTED EPILOGUE is a bonus book to be read after the series.

Buy Now

****

Standalones

Destroyed (Grey Romance)

She has a secret.
He has a secret.
One secret destroys them.

Buy Now

***

Unseen Messages (Survival Romance)

They crash landed together.
But if the island doesn't kill them.
Desire just might.

Buy Now

Made in United States
Troutdale, OR
08/05/2023

11838377R00127